Fight Me

Rivers Edge - Book 2

US Today Bestselling Author
Lacey Black

Lacey Black

Fight Me
Rivers Edge book 2

Lacey Black

Prologue

Erin

20 Years ago

I stand in front of my mirror, getting ready for my first day at yet another new school. My dad is a career officer in the military and it seems like every time I start to adjust to a new school, a new town, it's time for us to move on to someplace new.

I try to tame my frizzy red hair by pulling it back in a neon blue-and-green scrunchie that matches my favorite T-shirt with the rad dog and mountain of books. I push my large plastic glasses back up my lightly freckled nose and give myself one last look over. Well, seventh grade...here goes nothing.

My mom pulls up in front of Rivers Edge Junior High while kids run around and talk with all of their friends. "Do you want me to go in with you, sweetie?"

"No thank you, Mom. I can manage." I've been managing for a couple of years now. I'm lucky to make it through an entire grade at the same school before we're packing up and shuffling along to another town, another military base. Fortunately, my family doesn't have to live on base, but we have to be close enough for my dad to drive every day. Mom wanted a smaller town so they chose Rivers Edge, which is only a thirty minute drive to St. Charles for my dad.

"Okay, well, have a great first day, sweetie." Mom leans in and plants a kiss on my cheek. I pull away quickly as I throw open the passenger door on the family station wagon and pray no one saw that embarrassing display of affection. I step out and square my shoulders. Ready or not, Rivers Edge. Here I come.

I step into the busy halls of my new junior high school and look around for the office. Fortunately, it doesn't take me very long to locate it. Inside, there's a plump older secretary lecturing kids on running in the halls. She finishes her lecture and sends them on their way before noticing me for the first time, as I patiently wait in the back of the room.

"Can I help you?"

"I'm Erin Anderson. Today is my first day."

"Oh yes! Your mother enrolled you yesterday. I'm Mrs. Deany and we're so happy to have you with us at Rivers Edge Junior High, Erin. Here is your class schedule and your locker assignment. Lunch is at eleven thirty in the cafeteria and..." Mrs. Deany's voice trails off as she focuses her attention behind me. I turn around and get my first glimpse of the boy who just walked in the office. He's super tall with blond hair and pretty blue eyes. I can't help but stare at his striking features. He notices me staring at him and gives me the cockiest smile. I look away quickly and redirect my attention back to Mrs. Deany.

"Jake Stevens, what did you do this time?"

"Mrs. D, I didn't do anything. How could you possibly think I would do anything to warrant a trip to the office?" The boy, obviously named Jake, gives the secretary a big, charming grin as he strolls up to the counter next to where I'm standing.

"Oh, I don't know, Jake. Maybe because you are in this office at least twice a week?"

"Mr. Thomas was going to drop his books. I thought I'd be a stellar example to my fellow classmates and help him before he could drop them. It's not my fault he was caught off guard and tripped, spilling his coffee all over the books he was carrying and his starched white dress shirt." Another big smile comes from this boy, who apparently has more charm and charisma than any boy should be allowed to have.

"I'm sure it was a complete accident on your part that he spilled his coffee everywhere," she says, voice dripping with sarcasm.

"Completely not my fault. He was a little upset so he sent me down here to say hello to you."

"Jacob Stevens, what are we going to do with you?" Mrs. Deany sighs and rubs her forehead, fretting the start of a headache. She then turns her attention back to me. "I know what you're going to do. This is our new student, Erin. You are going to give her a quick tour of the school and show her where all of her classes are."

Jake gives me the once-over before his big smile returns to his face. "You got it, Mrs. D! Come on, darlin'. Let's go."

"Ten minutes and then you better be back in Mr. Thomas's class, Jake!" she yells as we head out the office doors into the now barren hallways.

I follow closely behind Jake. He's super tall compared to me and lanky, but not in that awkward way so many other junior high boys are. I'm lucky to hit five foot, but he seems to stand almost six foot tall already. I bet he plays basketball. He shows me the gym, the cafeteria, and the library. As we're heading back down the seventh grade hallway, he takes my schedule from me and starts to point out all my classes.

"Here's your English class. You're in my class. We have Miss Davenport. She's super fun when you get her all flustered." We continue walking the halls. "And over here is Math with Mr. Christianson. If you follow up everything he says with another question, you will make him cry. I've made that my life's mission in his class." We stop in front of a long row of lockers. "Here's your locker. Do you know how to open a combination lock?"

"Yes. This isn't my first school with lockers."

"How many schools have you been to?"

"Eight."

"Eight? Dang. That probably sucks. Here, let me throw your stuff in your locker for you." Jake takes my books and bag from my hands and does just that; throws it all in my locker. He pulls a pencil and a notebook from the mess he created and hands it back to me. "Here. Time to go to class."

"Don't you need anything?"

He laughs at me—actually laughs at my logical question. "Nope. I don't need anything. I have friends who take care of writing my notes for me."

"Friends?"

"Yep. Mostly girls. I could always use another friend to help me with my homework, if you're interested." He gives me another of those award-winning smiles and throws his arm over my shoulder.

"No thank you," I mumble, unable to keep the disgust out of my voice as I forcefully remove his arm from my shoulder.

"What's the matter? You don't like me? Everybody likes me. Everybody wants to be my friend."

"Well, not me. If you'll excuse me, I need to get to my first class." I try to walk around him but he steps to the side, blocking my effort. His eyes are so blue and full of mischief. I can almost see the wheels turning inside that cute little head of his.

"I think you *do* like me. That's your problem."

I feel the blush creeping into my cheeks. "Whatever. I need to go." Jake bends down and gets right in my face, the corner of his lip turned up in a partial smile. It's a beautiful smile.

"Welcome to Rivers Edge, Erin. I'll be seeing you very soon, darlin'," he says before he turns and walks away, assumingly toward his class. I stand there staring after him. He turns around suddenly, catching me watching him, and gives me a full-watt smile that makes my breath catch in my throat.

Oh, this boy is going to be trouble.

I've been in Rivers Edge for about four months already. I have developed a nice routine, which starts to scare me a little. Usually about the time I develop a routine, my parents announce my dad's being transferred again.

I've made friends with two girls who most will call geeks or nerds. We love books, don't mind homework, and love to study together. Sarah, Claire, and I meet up every day after school at the public library. It's my favorite place in this town. I could get lost in a library for days upon days, devouring book after book, story after story. Books are the one constant in my life. When everything around me changes, books are the same, offering me comfort in a world full of chaos and uncertainty.

I still see Jake every day, though it isn't because we're "friends." Jake is one of the popular kids and I am, well, *not*. I almost wish he would just ignore my existence. But he doesn't. He goes out of his way to say hi, wink at me, and offer to carry my books. It's almost like he's trying to embarrass me and keep me flustered.

The most embarrassing moment came one day, during study hall, when he proceeded to stand up on his seat and profess his undying love for me. His friends laughed and cheered him on as he humiliated me in front of thirty of our classmates. He received a detention for that stunt. But that embarrassing moment, as horrible as it was, was nothing compared to the humiliation I endured toward the end of March.

I was in a hurry to get to school on this rainy morning and was gathering up my books and notebooks from the desk in my room. What I didn't notice was I also grabbed my journal in my haste to get out the door. When you bounce around from town to town, school to school, everything in life becomes a big blur. I started a journal when I was in fifth grade and have faithfully kept it up. I write about my thoughts, my fears, my passions, things that transpire at school and at home, all the people in my life, including friends, classmates, teachers, parents, and most importantly, my crushes.

I am sitting in third period English, with Jake right behind me, and the room is quiet as we all take a test. What I didn't notice was Jake reaching into my satchel bag that is hanging on the back of my chair and pulling out my journal. Nor do I see him shove it in his own bag before the bell rang.

That night I search high and low for my journal. Where could I have put it? My journal is never out of my sight or out of its place on my desk. All night, I search the house for that thing—my most prized possession. *Everything* is in that journal.

The longer I search the more anxious I become, working myself up to the point of tears. So when it comes time to head to school the next morning, I am worn out and very moody.

As I walk in the front door of school, everyone is looking at me. No, it's not just a figment of my overactive seventh grade imagination. I mean, literally, everyone is looking at me. I try to keep my head down and walk to my locker. When I arrive, my friends Claire and Sarah are waiting for me with worried looks on their faces.

"What's wrong?" I ask.

"Umm, we have a slight problem," Sarah says in a low voice laced with worry.

"Okay, well you're starting to freak me out so just tell me."

Both girls share a look before Claire blurts out, "Jake stole your journal and showed it to everyone at school."

My entire world tilts on its axis. A buzzing sound starts in my ears as all the voices around me turn to laughter. Everyone is laughing at me. I look into the eyes of my only two friends in the world and know my life will never be the same. All the things I wrote about my parents, my classmates, my crushes—all out there for everyone to read and know. To judge. The tears start before I even realize they are sliding down my face.

"Don't cry, Erin. I'm sure it's not as bad as you think," Sarah says, even though I'm pretty sure even she doesn't believe her own words.

Kids walk around me at that moment dramatically proclaiming things like, "Ohhh, Jake. I love you!" and "My parents just don't understand me!"

Everyone is laughing and pointing, and I can't get my feet to work. They feel like they are stuck in wet concrete. I just look around the hallway, at the snickering faces of all my peers, and watch as they humiliate and ridicule at me.

Finally, Claire breaks my daze by yelling at those around us. Her words are enough for me to finally snap out of it and be able to move my feet. I take off running down the hall, and out the front door of the school.

"Erin, wait," I hear behind me. I know that voice. I've dreamed about that voice for months. It's Jake.

I turn around and face the one person who has managed to crush me into a million pieces. I expect to see him smiling and laughing with the rest of them, but he's not. He looks worried. Scared. "Where are you going?" he asks, voice laced with concern.

"Does it matter?" I snap. I turn to head toward the street, Jake still stands on the front steps of school.

"Erin! Wait!" I hear him yell as my legs carry me down the road and away from the school. "I'm sorry!"

I completely ignore him and don't stop running. I don't turn around to see if he's following me or if anyone is following me for that matter. I run as far as I can, until I can't run anymore. My legs are numb, my lungs are burning, and my throat is tight with emotion. I finally thought I'd found a place. A place where I actually fit in.

As I drop to my knees in the middle of the park, I cry for everything I'm about to lose. My friends. My house. My parents. Because there is no way I can or will stay in this town again. No way will I let people like Jake Stevens ever have this kind of power over me again. It's time for me to move on.

Chapter 1

Jake

Present Day

There's nothing worse than dressing up to shake hands with townsfolk just for the sake of being seen. But that's exactly what I'm doing on this Friday night, instead of heading to Jack's Pub and having a few drinks with my friends. Everyone in town will flock to the Rivers Edge Public Library for the retirement of ol' Mrs. Masterson.

Mabel Masterson has been the librarian in this town for forty-five years. Her marriage to her first husband didn't last six years, her second marriage only three years, and her third only a year. But here we are, dressing up to celebrate the only thing to put up with her for forty-five years. She's finally ready to hang up her reading glasses and step away from the library.

Mrs. Masterson is the stereotypical librarian. A petite little old lady who barely stands five foot tall with dark glasses that hang from a chain around her neck. Gray hair she wears in the same schoolmarm bun every day. Oh, and she's grumpy as hell. I'm pretty sure there isn't a person in Rivers Edge who doesn't toe the line when she's around. Why a woman like Mabel ever worked in a public place that deals with kids day in and day out, I'll never know.

So, why am I dressing up in a pair of khaki pants and a nice button-down shirt on my Friday night? Frankly, because Mabel is finally retiring at the ripe ol' age of seventy years old, and the town is having her retirement party this evening. Captain Edwards made it very clear that tonight was all-hands-on-deck. The mayor, town board, and all the highfalutin hobnobbers will be in attendance this evening, and it was ordered that all of us not on duty tonight were to be there too. Well, there's no way in hell they're getting me in a tie.

They're supposed to introduce the new librarian this evening. No one really knows who it is but the rumors are running wild. If Rivers Edge is known for anything, it's the fact everyone knows everything about everyone. Small town. In the past few weeks, I've heard she's almost as old as Mrs. Masterson, she's really a dude, and she's married with six kids. So who knows? Anything that involves the library generally has me turning a deaf ear, so I haven't even caught the new person's name. Not that I really care. I'm not exactly the library type.

I'm the drink a few beers on your day off, *Sports Center* watching type. At six foot three, I generally don't have trouble with the ladies. My eyes are the same color blue as most of my immediate family members, and my hair is a sandy-blond color. As a thirty-two-year-old veteran cop, I feel it's important to work out daily and run whenever I can. I pride myself on being in excellent physical shape, and that alone helps me to ensure I don't spend the evening alone if I don't want to.

I guess you could say I have a type of woman I generally stick with: tall with legs a mile long, hair color doesn't usually matter to me, and the bigger the chest, the better. I'm known around Rivers Edge as being a bit of a player since I don't date anyone longer than a few weeks. And, up until a few months ago, my best friend, Maddox, was my wingman. Now, instead of hitting the pub with me to score some babes, he's at home snuggling with my sister. Pussy.

I can't believe I'm heading to the library tonight. It's my weekend off, but it is booked solid. My sister, Avery, and Maddox, as well as my niece, Brooklyn, are moving into their new house this weekend. Not exactly how I wanted to spend my first weekend off in the new year, but they asked and I couldn't say no. Maddox has been my partner on the police force for ten years, and my best friend a hell of a lot longer. It was a pretty big shock to me when I found out before Thanksgiving that he was seeing my little sister behind my back.

Avery's had it rough the past few years. She dated this douchebag who ended up leaving her alone and pregnant. I thoroughly enjoyed punching him in the face, making sure he took the first swing so it didn't get me in trouble with my job. The only good to come out of their relationship was my niece, Brooklyn. I love that little girl like she's my own. She's the spitting image of my sister and has Maddox wrapped around her finger.

Maddox proposed to Avery a couple weeks back, on Christmas morning. Honestly, it still weirds me out a little, but there's no one better for my little sister than Maddox. He really is a good man with a huge heart, even if he is ten years older than she is. In the short time they've been together, I can tell how much he loves her. And as her oldest brother, that's all I've ever wanted for her and Brooklyn.

He put in an offer on the house of her dreams around Thanksgiving, and they closed on it last week. So here we are, the first weekend in the new year and I'm giving up my entire weekend to help them move in, well, me and my other brothers, Nate, Will, and Travis. If I know my parents at all, they'll be there helping; Mom bossing everyone around from the kitchen, and Dad entertaining Bean and keeping her out of the way.

Brooklyn's nickname was given to her at the hospital when she was born. Everyone argues over who came up with the nickname, and I'm pretty sure it was me. I am her favorite uncle, after all.

As I finish buttoning up the shirt I'm wearing for the evening, I text Maddox to confirm he's still coming to this shindig tonight.

Me: You're still coming, right?

Maddox: Yes. Cap will kill us if we don't show.

Me: I know. Do you think they'll have beer there?

Maddox: Uhhh, probably not. It's at the public library.

Me: Shit. I should drink before I go.

Maddox: Don't even think about it. You show up hungover tomorrow when we're moving, and your sister will kill both of us!

I chuckle out loud at the image of my five-foot-seven little sister getting in Maddox's face and letting him have it. She'd have to stand on a stepstool to even get close to his six-foot-plus frame, but she'd do it in a heartbeat. And he'd let her without as much as a word back at her. He's fucking whipped.

Me: You're right. I don't want to piss her off.

Maddox: Good man. See you in a little bit.

Me: Yep.

I slip my phone into my pocket and grab my keys before heading out my back door. My old 1986 Chevy pickup is in the driveway. I love this truck. I get my love for older cars and trucks from my dad. With his help about ten years ago, right after I was discharged from the military, I put a lot of time and money into bringing this truck back to life. I slide in the driver's seat, throw the shifter in reverse, and head out toward the library. This night is definitely going to suck.

I find a parking spot in the back of the full lot and head inside. People are everywhere, talking over the person next to them. I start to push my way through the crowd, but everyone here seems to want to chat. It takes me thirty minutes to even get into the main part of the library to find Maddox.

I see him standing against the far wall with a few of our fellow officers. I head in their direction, trying to avoid making eye contact with anyone else so I don't get stopped. I keep my head down and barrel through the crowd.

When I finally get over to the guys, we all shake hands. "You ready for the move tomorrow?" I ask Maddox.

"Yeah, I think so. My house has been boxed up for a couple of weeks now, since I've been staying over at Avery's. I put Brooklyn to bed tonight so Avery could stay up and finish all the last-minute packing. I think we'll be all ready to go by eight when everyone is supposed to get there."

"I'll be there by eight, maybe earlier. You gonna have coffee ready?"

"Of course. Not saying we'll be able to find the cups, but the coffee pot is the last thing Avery's planning on packing." Maddox smiles at the mention of his fiancée's name.

"All right. Did James call you?"

"Yep. He's taking his pickup and trailer to my place. Will and Travis are going to meet him there and work on loading up my house. Nate is coming to Avery's and the three of us will work on her place."

"Sounds like you have it planned out pretty well. I threw my tie-down straps in the bed of the truck tonight so I should be ready for tomorrow. Anything else you can think of that I should bring?"

"Nope. I don't think so. Sunday is when I'll need the most help."

"More help than all the manual labor you're getting tomorrow?"

Maddox smiles at me. "Yep. Sunday we're putting together the man cave."

Ah, yes. The man cave. It's my favorite feature in the house he bought for Avery. There's a large room and shop on the back of their two-car garage that is perfect for a couch, big-screen television, fridge, and maybe a pool table. It's the room I look forward to frequenting as much as I can.

Just then someone thumps a microphone and encourages the crowd to quiet down. Mayor Thorsten is standing at the front of the library by the front desk at a makeshift podium. "Good evening, fine citizens of Rivers Edge. So glad you could all join us this evening." The crowd gives him a round of applause.

"Tonight, we are honoring the forty-five years of service Mrs. Mabel Masterson has given to the fine folks of Rivers Edge." Mabel is standing up next to the mayor, scowling at the crowd there to honor her. "Mabel has dedicated her life to serving you all in the educational capacity and has turned our fine library into a wonderful place to read and learn. Mabel, would you like to say something?" He turns and looks at Mabel, who in turn gives him a sour look like she just sucked on a lemon.

"Well, then, thank you for all coming this evening and helping wish Mabel Masterson a happy retirement." Another round of applause.

"And now, I'd like to introduce Mabel's replacement as librarian. She's no stranger to our fine town, having lived here for part of a year during her youth. She comes to us from Jackson, Mississippi, where she's been an assistant librarian for the past four years. Please help me welcome, Miss Erin Anderson."

The applause around me fades away until I can't hear anything. I stare at the front of the library as Erin, *my* Erin, walks up to stand next to Mayor Thorsten. What the hell? Erin is the new librarian?

"Thank you, Mayor Thorsten. I look forward to getting reacquainted with the residents of Rivers Edge and continuing the fine service this library offers the community." Her voice is light and happy. Her fiery red hair is barely contained by a clip, and her emerald green eyes scan the crowd. She has a big smile on her face that only seems to enhance her beauty. I can't help but stare at the simple radiance of this woman. The woman I've barely stopped thinking about since the day I ran into her in the grocery store last fall.

"Thank you all for coming tonight, everyone," she says as she waves and starts to walk away from the podium. I continue to watch her as she scans the crowd, taking in all the faces in front of her. But when her green eyes slam into mine, my chest tightens and my breath catches in my throat. Her startled green eyes quickly look away as she walks toward a woman and begins talking.

I continue to stare at her, watching as she chats with townsfolk. She glances up once and my equally surprised eyes lock with hers. I couldn't look away from her if I tried. She quickly diverts her attention back to those she's speaking with. I turn back to Maddox; the smiling, very smug face of my best friend.

"See something you like, my friend?"

"Screw you. I don't know what you're talking about," I mumble.

"Sure you don't," he says as he slaps my back and chuckles. "Just so you know, I said the same thing when I was fighting my feelings for your sister." With that he turns and walks away.

I stand here for a moment, watching his retreating back as he heads toward another group of people. Out of all the people in Rivers Edge, I finally find someone I can't get out of my head. Someone who invades my thoughts day and night. Someone who, apparently, still hates my guts. Erin Anderson. What the hell do I do now?

Chapter 2

Erin

It's been the longest night of shaking hands and making small talk. There are only a few faces I actually remember from all those years ago when I lived that short time in Rivers Edge. But of all those faces, the one I remember the most was staring at me half the night: Jake Stevens.

I've managed to avoid him over the last couple of months since my arrival in town. Well, with the exception of that time in the grocery store. He didn't even remember who I was. That should tell me exactly what kind of person he is. He doesn't care whose life he tried to ruin in school. Okay, so maybe I'm being a little dramatic. Fine. But seeing Jake tonight—in my library of all places—has my stomach all in knots and my brain a little out of whack.

I decide to help the caterers clean up the messes on the tables and around on the bookshelves that were left by all the residents of Rivers Edge who stopped by tonight. Honestly, I am a little surprised by the number of people who showed up. I remember how grumpy and impersonal Mabel Masterson was when I was in school here twenty years ago, and she definitely hasn't changed any. I've spent the past two months learning the ins and outs of the library from her. Getting her to talk to me was like pulling teeth. I guess I'm just going to have to learn as I go. Trial by fire? No problem. I'm up for it!

As I drag the garbage can to the next table, I catch bits and pieces of a conversation behind me. I know whose voice it is, but I choose at this moment to ignore him. If I don't acknowledge him, maybe he'll just go away?

"Hey, Erin. Good to see you again. I know I've said it before, but welcome back to Rivers Edge." I turn to face Maddox Jackson, who is sliding his coat on, apparently ready to head out the door. He's standing with a few guys who look familiar, but I can't think of their names, and Jake.

"Thanks for coming, Maddox. I'll see you around," I say as I turn back to the table I'm clearing.

I hear Jake say goodbye to his friends, but I don't turn around again to see who from the group is actually leaving. *Don't turn around. Don't you dare turn around.*

"So, a librarian, huh?"

Don't turn around. "Yep," I say, still trying to focus all of my attention on clearing the plates and cups from the table.

"I can see that about you."

"What does that mean?" I ask defensively as I whip around to face him. I didn't realize how close he was to me. We're standing barely a foot apart. My eyes go wide with the realization that we're so close. I look up and up into his stunning blue eyes. He's taller than I remember him, definitely over six feet. Depending on what shoes I'm wearing or whether or not you're looking at my driver's license, I'm just a handful of inches over the five-foot mark. My hands fling to my hips, taking a defiant stance, ready to do battle with Jake Stevens.

"Nothing," he says with both arms up, as if waving the white flag in surrender. "I just meant I could see you as a librarian. You always liked reading and books."

I turn my attention back to the table I was clearing. "You know nothing about me, Jake."

He sighs and is quiet for a few moments. I start to think maybe he has gotten the hint and walked away. "You're right. I know nothing about you. Anymore. I used to know you."

"Even then, you knew nothing about me. You *thought* you knew me twenty years ago, based on a few months of school and a few small encounters. I wasn't your friend then, and I'm not your friend now." I realize I've been wiping the same spot over and over again, but I can't seem to calm down enough to do another task.

He's quiet as he stands behind me. I hear him clear his throat before he says, "You're right. Good night, Erin." Then he turns around and walks out of the library.

I'm left standing here, looking at the place he just stood, and wondering if I'll ever really get over Jake Stevens. It's not like I'm in love with him or anything. I just don't know if I will ever get past the hurt and anger I've carried around with me for twenty years. And for the first time in the past two months, I question whether coming back to Rivers Edge was the right choice.

After all the patrons have left, all the food is cleaned up and removed, and the doors are locked up for the night, it's finally time for me to head home. Tomorrow is the first official day that I take over as librarian. I'm excited and a little nervous knowing Mrs. Masterson won't be around to answer any questions I may have. Though, she didn't really help answer my questions before, so I guess it's really just another day at the office.

I pull into the driveway of the large house I've been renting for the past few months and kill the engine. I got this old house for a steal after Mr. Johnson passed away last spring. Mrs. Johnson couldn't keep up with the day-to-day upkeep of the large house, and her family finally convinced her to move into assisted living care.

I've been putting all of my free time and extra money into updating some things around the place. I've painted almost every room, which already breathes new life into the old, worn-out home. I've also painted the cabinets in the kitchen, updated lighting fixtures, and purchased new outlet covers. I have a handful of new outlets, but I'm not ready to tackle those by myself just yet. I'll find someone who knows a little about electrical and pay them to help me. Eventually, I'd love to rip up the old carpeting in the living room and refinish the hardwood floors underneath, but that's still a little ways out there. All in all, I think I'm doing pretty well learning new home improvement skills thanks to a couple of how-to books I found at the library.

I walk in the familiar front door and deposit my work satchel down on the foyer table. I was also lucky the Johnsons left a ton of furniture for me to rummage through. The vintage, eclectic furnishings fit right in with the older home charm. I hear the soft "meow" before I see my Siamese cat, Miss Whiskers, stroll in from the living room. She arches her back and stretches like I just busted her from one of her many daily naps. She's a lazy cat, but I love her all the same.

"Hi, Miss Whiskers. Did you miss me today?" I ask as I pick my kitty up off the old floor and rub my nose along the top of her soft head, nuzzling her pointed ears.

I rescued Miss Whiskers from a shelter back in Jackson, Mississippi, where I was living prior to coming to Rivers Edge. I was a resident of Jackson for almost twenty years before I finally decided to broaden my horizons and move away from the only place I've ever really called home. It was the hardest decision I've ever had to make, but I'm comfortable with the changes, the move, and my life in Rivers Edge.

I love snuggling up to Miss Whiskers; the feel of her heart beating against my chest and the sound of her joyous purrs. I've never considered myself a cat person. Heck, I've never been able to have a pet before, not even a fish. When I was younger and moving around so much, my parents didn't want to deal with a pet on top of relocating. So, as soon as I was living on my own, I went to the shelter and adopted my baby girl.

I walk into my kitchen and set Miss Whiskers down on the floor by her dish. There's still a little water in her dish, but she's out of food. Miss Whiskers is a high maintenance cat – only eats fancy wet food. I've tried to break her of this eating habit, but every time I put dry food in her bowl, she refuses to eat any of it and just meows as loud as she possibly can. Yep, she's a food snob.

Miss Whiskers starts to meow at me as I step over to the sink to top off her water bowl. When I get to the counter, I slip on the floor, almost falling down.

"What in the world?" I open the cabinet under the sink and see the water streaming down from the old pipe. "Great!"

I reach into a drawer and pull out all the hand towels I have and lay them out on the floor to soak up the water. What do I do now? I search my memory for anything in those how-to books that talked about water leaks. Nothing. I have no idea what to do so I grab a large bowl and stick it under the leak. There. Done.

Except I can't leave it like this all night.

I really don't want to call a plumber at this point on a Friday night, knowing it will cost a higher overnight or weekend rate. Mrs. Johnson's daughter won't be able to help me, and she lives forty-five minutes away anyway. The only person I can think of to call for help is Maddox. He gave me his phone number when I ran into him at the hardware store a couple of months back, offering his help anytime I might need it. Well, I think this qualifies.

I grab my phone and pull up his number. I cringe when I look up at the clock on the stove and notice it's well after ten o'clock. It is ringing for the third time and I start to get nervous, ready to hang up. Maybe he's already asleep? I'm calling later than I ever wanted to call anyone's house, knowing they have a family at home sleeping.

"Hello?" a woman answers, sounding very tired.

"Good evening. This is Erin Anderson, and I'm so sorry to call so late at night. Is Maddox available by chance?"

"He's right here. Hold on a second, Erin." I hear muffled voices talking and assume she puts her hand over the phone while she talks to Maddox.

"Hello?"

"Hi, Maddox. I'm so, so sorry for calling you so late at night, but I have a little problem."

"It's okay, Erin. I'm still up packing for our move tomorrow. What's up?"

That's right! I recall overhearing conversations tonight that he was moving in with Jake's little sister tomorrow. "Well, I came home from the retirement party tonight and my kitchen floor was soaked. My sink is leaking water all over the place, and I don't really know what to do."

"Do you have a bucket you can put under the leak?"

"Yeah, I have a big bowl under there now."

"Okay, good. I'm not really sure what to do without looking at the leak to determine if maybe you just have a busted fitting or something more serious with the pipe itself. I have a friend, James, who actually lives not too far from you. Why don't I give him a call and see if he can buzz over and check it out for you?"

"Oh, you don't have to do that. I just didn't know if there was something I could do without having to call a plumber."

"Well, it may be an easy fix, but I'm just not sure. I know James well, and I'm sure he can give you a little advice. I'd run over myself, but I'm afraid Avery will kill me if I leave this disaster for her to tackle alone." He chuckles as his fiancée mouths off in the background.

"Well, if you think he could help. I'd be willing to pay him."

"I'll call him and call or text you back."

"Thank you so much, Maddox. Tell Avery thank you for taking the call, and again, I'm so sorry for disturbing you all so late at night."

"Don't worry about it, Erin. We're happy to help. Talk to you soon."

"Thanks again. Bye." I hang up the phone and sit back and wait on my plumbing knight to come and rescue me. Heck, maybe James is cute and it won't be such a bad thing that my pipes started leaking in the middle of the night.

A text comes through my phone a few minutes later.

Maddox: Help is on the way!

Excellent! James is coming to help so I should probably get to cleaning up the excess water standing on my kitchen floor.

Chapter 3

Jake

I'm relaxing on my couch in a pair of sweatpants when my phone rings. Maddox.

"Don't tell me you can't wait for my help until tomorrow. I'm not coming over now to pack up boxes, dude."

"No, I need your help with something else."

"What?"

"Erin just called and her kitchen sink is leaking." I sit straight up on my couch at the sound of her name. "I called James to see if he could run over there to help her, but he's up at Jack's. Can you run over there?"

"Don't ever call James again before you call me when it comes to Erin," I growl into the phone. "I'm on my way." I hear Maddox laughing as I click off the phone without even saying goodbye.

Dick.

I head back to my bedroom to grab a sweatshirt and some socks. Once my feet are stuffed in my running shoes, I grab my keys and head out the back door toward my garage. I grab a few hand tools I might need for a water leak and throw them in the cab of my truck. I'm out of the drive and heading toward Erin's a few minutes later. Yes, James may live a couple of blocks away, but there is no way in hell I'm going to allow that douche to help Erin. If anyone is going to go over there in the middle of the night, it's going to be me.

I decide to leave the tools until I know what I'm dealing with, so I step out of the truck and head up the front steps. The porch light is on, which means she's aware of my pending arrival.

She opens the door after I knock and the look on her face is one of pure shock. While she stands before me, mouth gaping open, eyes wide with surprise, I take in the image in front of me. Erin has changed out of her proper librarian sweater and slacks and is standing in her doorway wearing form fitting sweats, a green tank top, and nothing covering her bright pink toes. Her red curls are pulled up in a messy ponytail and the little bit of makeup she had on earlier is gone. I can't help but look her up and down—and back up again—taking in the slender, yet curvy body in front of me. She's sexy as hell, and I feel myself thickening in my sweats.

"What are you doing here?" she finally spits out, shock still evident all over her face.

I look down at her again, noticing this time the very cold outside air is making her nipples hard through her bra. My eyes are glued to her perky chest—a chest she usually hides behind baggy mom-clothes—and I have to fight the urge to groan. I'm hard as steel and don't even care that I'm wearing sweatpants and pitching a tent to rival any Boy Scouts' campsite.

Erin's eyes follow mine and she realizes what I'm staring at. Her arms quickly whip up and she lays them across her chest, covering herself up. She then glances down at my pants and gasps. Her eyes fly up to my face, a deep red blush spreading up her neck to her cheeks. Her big green eyes are glued to mine. A cocky smile spreads across my lips, which causes her eyes to turn venomous.

"I said, what are you doing here, Jake?" she snaps, eyes shooting daggers.

I return my focus back on her face and notice she's shivering. "You're cold. Can we go inside and talk about it?"

Lacey Black

She hesitates but steps back to allow me access. I step inside, taking in the older home she's obviously put some work into recently.

"Jake."

"Maddox called me and said you had a leak."

"I thought James was coming."

"You were going to answer the door half naked for James?" I can't hide the irritation in my voice.

"I'm not half naked! I was cleaning up the water mess in the kitchen. I'm completely covered." She turns away from me, ponytail flipping over her shoulder, and walks toward the kitchen.

I follow her to the kitchen, taking in the soft yellow cabinets and the blue walls. The cabinet under the sink is open, a large bowl catching the dripping water, and towels spread out all over the floor. I don't even hesitate, I crouch down on my knees on the wet floor in front of the open cabinet. I pinpoint right away what the problem is.

"Looks like you have a busted fitting. Your pipes are pretty old. I'm surprised you haven't had more problems than this."

"Well, I haven't been here long enough yet. It's only been about two months."

"I need to run out to my truck and grab a few tools," I say as I stand up, sweatpants wet at the knees, and walk toward the front door. My mind is filled with the repeating image of Erin answering her door with pink toes and a tank top clad chest. Shit, I need to focus or I'll never fix her problem. All I want to do right now is fix *my* problem in my pants.

When I get back inside, Erin is scooping up the wet towels and throwing them in the washing machine, just off of the kitchen. She tries holding her arms away from her body, but it doesn't work completely. Her tank top is now wet and stuck against her body. It might be the sexiest damn thing I've ever seen.

I clear my throat and force myself to look away and back to the task at hand. I grab a wrench and get to work on shutting off the water valve under the sink. After a few minutes of checking, I can confirm the fitting holding two pipes together is rusted and leaking water.

"So, I have good news and I have bad news," I say as I stand back up and face Erin.

"Good news first."

"Well, you have a rusty fitting and it needs to be replaced. It's a pretty easy, quick fix that won't cost you but a couple of bucks." I wipe my wet hands on the towel she hands me.

"That's good. So, what's the bad news?"

"The hardware store is closed for the night so I won't be able to change it until tomorrow for you. I had to shut off the water to the sink so you won't be able to use it until it's fixed."

Erin blows out a big breath and looks around the room. "You don't have to do that, Jake. I can have someone else do it tomorrow."

"Who?" I glare down at her, meeting her challenge head-on.

She crosses her arms defiantly. "I'll call James."

"James? I don't think so." I mimic her stance; feet firmly apart, arms crossed at my chest.

"You have *no* say in what I do here or who I call for help, Jake."

"No, but I'll be damned if James is coming over to help you. I'll stop by the hardware store on my way over and get a new fitting for the pipe." With that I start picking up my tools and head toward the door.

She storms after me, bare feet slapping against the hardwood floor. "What if I'm not going to be here tomorrow? You can't just boss me around and expect me to bend to your every whim."

"Where are you going to be?" I ask as I turn back around to face her, her emerald green eyes are as dark and smoky as night.

"None of your business," she replies, chin firmly up in the air.

I lean forward until my face is within a few inches of hers. "Well, I've made it my business, darlin'. And you could thank me for coming over here in the middle of the night and getting my pants all wet from crawling all over your floor, all just to help you out."

I can see the fire extinguish a little in her eyes. Her face softens and her eyes return to their normal bright green color. "I'm sorry. You're right. Thank you for helping me tonight, Jake."

I give her a half smile and say, "Oh, you're welcome, darlin'. I'll let you make it up to me very soon." She snaps back to attention and gives me a cold look. "I'll see you tomorrow, darlin'." And then I turn and walk out her door.

I hear her open the door behind me. "And quit calling me that!"

I chuckle as I throw my tools into the passenger side of my truck and hop in. Erin is standing in the window, arms crossed over her perky chest, scowl still evident on her beautiful face.

Oh yes, Erin. I will definitely see you tomorrow...and I will *never* quit calling her that.

Saturday morning proves to be one big pain in the ass. I head over to Avery's by seven thirty to make sure everything is ready to go for the move. When I walk through the front door, I hear the little feet of my niece, Brooklyn.

"Uncle Jake! You here!"

"I'm here, Bean," I exclaim as I pick her up and give her a big kiss. "How's my favorite little lady doing today?"

"We're moving!"

"Yes, you are. By the way, who's your favorite uncle?" I ask with a grin.

"You," she giggles. "Mommy says I can have a puppy!"

"Really? Well, next time you are at my house, we'll go pick one out!"

"YAY! Daddy, Uncle Jake says I can pick a puppy when I stay wiff him!"

"Thank you very much, Jake," Maddox says sarcastically as he walks into the room.

"Hey, that's what friends and uncles are for."

"I'll remember that," he smarts off as he turns and heads into the kitchen. He pours three cups of coffee and hands me one. I watch as he walks over to the fridge and grabs the milk, pouring just a splash in the third cup that is still sitting on the counter.

Maddox looks up at my smiling face. "What?"

"So, when did you lose your balls? Does Avery carry them around in her purse and give them back to you for special occasions?"

"Fuck you! I didn't lose anything. My balls are still firmly attached where they've always been."

"That's right, honey. They're very much where they've always been," Avery says as she walks in and grabs a hold of Maddox's junk. Seriously.

"What the hell was that? I thought I told you not to even touch each other when I'm around," I thunder across the kitchen at my sister.

She smiles over her shoulder at me before placing a kiss on her fiancé's lips.

"Don't be a hater, my friend. Coming home every night to my smokin' hot fiancée is the best part of my day."

I grumble a little under my breath. "Whatever. I just don't want you feeling each other up in front of me. I'm going to have nightmares."

"Oh, Jake. You are not as tough as you think you are. Someday, someone is going to come along and knock you down a few pegs. I can't wait to sit back and watch it happen."

"Not happening."

"Oh, speaking of not happening, whatever happened last night at Erin's?" Maddox inquires with a smug look on his cocky face.

I want to punch him.

"Oh, that's right. Did she get her leak fixed?" Avery asks while sipping her coffee.

"I need to stop by the hardware store and grab a new fitting before I run over to her place and fix her up."

"Wait, you went over there?" Avery turns toward Maddox now. "I thought you were calling James?"

"I did, but James was uptown at Jack's. Jake was next on the list," Maddox defends.

"Yeah, but don't you and Erin have bad history?" Avery asks as she points a finger in my direction.

"Not so much a history as we went to school together for a little bit."

Maddox snorts and says, "Yeah, a history that ended with her leaving school and this town after you humiliated her in front of the whole school." I glare at my best friend for bringing it up in front of my sister.

"I heard all about what you did, Jake. You were horribly mean to her. I'm surprised she's even talking to you."

"Oh, she's not. She hates I'm even around her. But that's kind of the fun part. She gets all flustered and angry at me. It's actually kind of hot," I say with a smirk as I finish my coffee.

"Well, I think you may have actually met your match, Jake Stevens. I can't wait to see her bring you to your knees," Avery says with a huge smile spread across her face.

"Anyway, let's get this show on the road. Where's Nate?" I ask as I turn to rinse my cup in the sink.

"Right here," I hear as Nate walks through the front door. He goes over to Brooklyn and gives her a big hug before joining us in the kitchen. "What did I miss?"

"Oh, Jake is in love with someone who wants nothing to do with him. It's awesome," Avery spits out before I can say anything. Nate's eyebrow rises to the ceiling and a big smug smile crosses his face.

"Really?"

"No. Avery's being dramatic. I am *not* in love with anyone nor do I want to be."

"The best part about love, Jake, is that you don't get to pick when it happens. It just does," Avery replies with another big smile across her face. She walks over to Maddox and puts her arm around his waist; his arm goes protectively around her shoulders.

"Whatever, Avery. I'm not in love. End of story."

"Who are we talking about here?" Nate inquires.

"Erin Anderson," Maddox replies.

"Oh, you mean the hot new librarian? The guys at the firehouse were talking about how smoking' hot she is. Plus, I hear she's single." My ears start to burn and I can't stop the anger that starts to well up in my chest. I want to walk over and punch my fucking brother right now.

"She is single from what I've gathered. You should give her a call sometime, Nate," Maddox throws out there with a huge smile. Maddox is just trying to piss me off now, and I try to not respond. I don't want to give him the satisfaction of seeing me squirm. But, when I look over at Nate, who is smiling at Maddox, and says, "Maybe I'll do that." – I can't stop the words from flying from my lips.

"Don't you dare. If anyone is calling Erin, it's going to be me," I respond in a low, menacing growl.

All three of them are looking at me with huge self-righteous smiles on their faces. "Well, that didn't take him long to admit," Avery says as she goes about cleaning up the coffee mess and packing it all up in the final box.

"Shut the hell up, all of you. We have boxes to move. Let's get going." I turn to walk in the living room, leaving the three of them laughing at me behind my back. Assholes.

I am flat-out exhausted come three o'clock. After we move the very last box, the very last piece of furniture to Maddox and Avery's new house, I'm ready to go home and grab a beer. I pride myself on my physical appearance, running several times a week and playing softball when I can during the summer, but that move was brutal. Even basic training in the military didn't seem to have anything on that move. Remind me to never offer to help someone who has stairs ever again.

Mom cooked a quick meal for all of us over at Avery's new place, but before I can kick back and relax, I have to run to the hardware store and fix Erin's sink.

After making the quick stop at Peterson Hardware, I set out toward Erin's house. When I pull in, I don't see her car anywhere. When I go up and knock, it goes unanswered. Where in the hell is she? She knows I'm coming over.

Thirty minutes later, her little red Volkswagen Bug pulls up behind my truck.

"Where have you been?" I ask before she's even out of the car.

"Uh, I had stuff to do at the library today."

"Well, I told you I was going to stop by and fix your sink," I say as she starts to open her front door.

"Well, you never told me what time you were coming over. I had stuff to do. I'm not just going to sit here and wait around for you all day." She throws the door open and sets her purse and keys down on the entry table, tossing her coat over the top of her purse.

She turns around, hands on her hips, and stares up at me with as much defiance as she can muster. She looks hot when she gets all worked up. Hell, she looks hot period. She's standing there in tight jeans and a fitted blue sweater. Her red hair is down with big ringlets of curls framing her face. She's still wearing very little makeup, but what she is wearing accentuates her big green eyes. God, she's beautiful when she's mad.

"I didn't know what time I was going to be here," I reply as I head toward her kitchen, leaving her standing in the foyer.

I hear her feet practically stomping after me as I reach the kitchen sink. "Jake."

I turn to face her, arms crossed over my chest. She's standing nose to nose—or, actually, nose to chest since I'm a foot taller than she is—with me, arms still resting on her hips. "Yes, Erin?"

"You are without a doubt *the* most frustrating person I've ever met! You can't just come in here and make yourself at home, bossing me around like you own the place!"

As I'm standing mere inches from this petite little fireball, I have the overwhelming urge to kiss the shit out of her. I have to fight myself to keep my arms crossed at my chest. My fingers are itching and twitching to dive into her hair. I can't help the smirk that crosses my lips as I say, "You're really hot when you're mad, you know that?"

"Uhhhhhhhh!" Erin throws her hands up in the air and stomps out of the room. The last thing she hears as she leaves the room is the sound of my laughter.

Chapter 4

Erin

Seriously! How can one person be so pigheaded and narrow-minded? He doesn't own me. I owe him nothing. Okay, so maybe that's not entirely correct. He is downstairs changing the fitting on my sink so, at the very least, I owe him a thank you.

After leaving Jake to his task at hand, I escape to my home office to check my email. This is the only room I haven't really worked on yet. I have so many things I want to do to really make it the perfect home office and library, but really have no idea where to start.

As I sit down and boot up my email, I see the first one is from my mom. My mom has been contacting me through email lately, which works fine for me because then I'm not stuck on the phone listening to her whine about my dad's snoring or their strokes over par in golf.

When Dad finally retired from the military, they relocated to Florida and purchased a condo on a golf course. Neither one of them played golf, but they felt they deserved the full retirement lifestyle as a way of making up for their constant moving and relocating practically their entire adult lives. I am happy they finally settled down somewhere. It's just a shame that it was never with me.

I hear a knock on the door and look up from my laptop. Jake

is standing in the doorway, wiping his hands on a rag.

"All done."

"Okay." I stand up, set Miss Whiskers down on the floor, shut the laptop lid, and walk around my desk to stand in front of him. He's somewhere around a foot taller than me so I have to look up to make eye contact. "Listen, Jake. I really appreciate your help in fixing the sink. You probably saved me a bunch of money by not having to call a plumber on the weekend. So, thank you."

Jake's crystal-blue eyes burn into mine. He's quiet for several moments and I start to wonder if he's going to talk at all, acknowledge anything I just said. I'm beginning to get antsy and nervous as I look at this extremely good-looking guy standing in my office. He really is hot. Too bad he's a total tool.

"I have an idea. How about to say thank you, you come with me to Avery and Maddox's new place for dinner. My mom's been cooking up a storm all afternoon and has a big spread planned."

"Oh, I couldn't do that. That's your family time."

"Don't worry about that. Mom always makes plenty of food. And besides, there were a few other guys who helped them move today so they'll be there too."

I mull it over in my head for a few moments. I'd love to go and see the rest of Jake's family, since it has been nearly twenty years. Jake's mom was super nice to me that afternoon my parents and Jake's parents met up to discuss the issue at school. But do I really want to be that close to Jake? Do I really want to put myself through more of his torture? "I have some work I need to do here at home, and—" Jake cuts me off before I can finish my sentence.

"Don't say no, Erin. You're new in town and probably don't know too many people. You can hang out with and get to know my sister, Avery."

The thought of spending some time with another female does sound awfully nice right now. "Are you sure they won't mind?"

"No way. My mom's a big fan of the saying 'the more the merrier.'"

"Well, if you think they won't mind, then okay."

"Great. I'll meet you at the front door." With that, Jake turns and walks out of the office.

What did I just get myself into? I stand here in my office for a few minutes and try to collect my thoughts. I can't believe I am going to have dinner with Jake's family.

When I walk into the foyer, Jake is patiently waiting by the door with his tools. "Ready to go?"

"I can drive myself. I'll just follow you to their place."

"Why? We're both going to the same place."

"I don't need you to shuttle me around. I can drive."

"I'm not denying you couldn't drive yourself. Why would you want to? Just get in my truck."

"This isn't a date. If I want to leave, then I can."

"Why would you want to leave?"

"Why do you keep countering everything I say with a question?"

"Why do you insist on fighting me every step of the way?"

"You are the most stubborn man I know, and I'm so tired of you thinking you know everything!"

"I'm stubborn!?"

"Absolutely! If it's not *your* way, then it's the wrong way!"

Jake lets out a low growl and bends down to get right in my face. "Honey, *your* way is the most ass-backwards way I've ever seen! You want to fight with me just for the sake of fighting."

"Maybe it's your approach. Did you ever think of that?"

"What the hell is wrong with my approach?" Jake is standing at his truck, passenger door open, as if waiting on me to jump in.

"You don't ask. You assume or boss. I'm not someone you can just *tell* what to do and I'll do it. Maybe you should try asking, Jake. How about that?" I say, arms defiantly crossed at my chest.

Jake lets out a loud sigh and drops his arms to his side. "Erin, why don't we just ride together to my sister's house? I'd be happy to drop you back off at home here when we're done."

I stand here, looking at him for a few heartbeats before I answer, "Okay. As long as you're okay with dropping me back off when we're done." With that I hop up in the cab of his old pickup.

He's staring at me, mouth gaping open. "Really? Just like that? I ask, you answer, and hop up in my truck like it was no big deal?"

"It's your approach, Jake. Ask and you shall receive," I say with a semi-sweet smile on my face.

Jake shakes his head as he shuts the passenger door. I watch him walk around the cab of the truck and hop in the driver's seat. He looks over at me one more time and shakes his head again.

"You drive me crazy," he says under his breath.

"Well, don't worry. The feeling is completely mutual," I reply loudly. He throws his truck in reverse and heads out toward Avery's new house. What did I just get myself into?

When we reach what I assume is our final destination, Jake has to park down the street because of all the cars and trucks. The house is stunning. It's big and has two huge bay windows on the front porch. I could definitely get comfortable in a house like this. You can hear the noise from down the block. It definitely sounds like there's a party going on at this house.

A little girl of maybe three or four comes running out the front door when we approach the steps. "Uncle Jake!"

"Bean, what the heck are you doing out here without a coat on? Your mom is going to be very upset if you get sick. Do you remember how you had to go to the hospital a few months back when you got sick?" Jake picks up the little blue-eyed blonde and snuggles her into his chest as he hurries inside the house.

"Who dat?"

"This is my friend, Erin. Can you say hi to her?"

"Hi."

"Hi. And what is your name?"

"Bwookwyn."

"Brooklyn is a beautiful name. It's so nice to meet you," I say as Jake sets his niece back down on the floor. He removes his coat and starts to make a grab for the collar of my coat.

"I can do it," I say as I shake his hands off of my coat.

"Fine. Just thought I'd be nice and help."

"You can try asking. You might get farther."

Before Jake can respond, we are joined in the foyer by an older version of the woman I met twenty years ago. "Erin Anderson, is that you, dear?" Mrs. Steven says as she leans forward and gives me a gentle motherly hug.

"Hi, Mrs. Stevens. It's so nice to see you again."

"Oh, please call me Elizabeth. I'm so glad you are joining us for dinner. It'll be ready in just a few moments."

"Well, thank you for having me. I know it's sort of sudden, but..."

"Oh, you just hush, dear. We always have plenty of food to go around. I'm used to making large meals for my growing boys and their friends," she says as she pats Jake's stomach.

"Why don't you come into the kitchen with me and Avery, and Jake can go help the guys move the furniture in the living room."

"Mom," Jake says in a tone laced with warning.

"Jake, don't you worry, honey. We'll be just fine without you." She gives me a wink as she steers me toward the kitchen. "I think he's afraid I'm going to show you his naked baby pictures or tell you all about his embarrassing moments as a child," she says with a grin. "It'll have to wait until you come to my house, dear. I just don't carry them all with me anymore."

I can't help but laugh. If I was going to be spending more time with this family, I could definitely see myself enjoying my time with

Mrs. Stevens. But I don't plan on it. I don't plan on spending any more time with Jake Stevens. Well, except for tonight. But it's just a way of saying thanks for helping me with my sink. After tonight, no more time with Jake.

"Mom, all the side salads are out. Oh, I'm sorry. Who's this?" A beautiful blonde several inches taller than me is standing at the kitchen island removing lids from a bunch of plastic bowls.

"This is Erin Anderson. She came with Jake." I sense the happiness in her voice as she tells her daughter.

"Jake invited me over since he just finished fixing my sink. I'm not *with* Jake," I defend.

Avery looks at me with a big smile on her face. "I like this one already."

"Me too, honey," Mrs. Stevens adds with a coy smile.

I stand here staring at the two ladies in front of me feeling like there's something more going on here.

"What?" I finally ask.

"Oh nothing, dear. Jake just never brings girls to family dinners."

"Like never," Avery adds. "The last girl he brought over was that tramp in college. You remember her, Mom? The one who was hitting on Nate by the end of the night?"

"Of course I remember, dear. But that has nothing to do with the now." Mrs. Stevens turns her attention back to me as she goes about final preparations for the meal. "So, Erin. What have you been up to since we saw you last?"

"Well, after I left Rivers Edge, I went to live with my grandma in Jackson, Mississippi. I graduated there and then went on to college earning my Master's in Library Science. I'm still in touch with a friend I went to school with here, so when she mentioned Mrs. Masterson was retiring, I decided to check into the position. I loved it in Jackson but after my grandma died, I realized I wanted to return to a smaller town. So here I am."

"Oh, I'm sorry to hear about the loss of your grandmother.

But, I'll be honest, we are so glad you are back. You were always the nicest child."

"Yeah, until Jake ruined her," Avery replies. My heart starts to beat a little faster and my palms start to sweat. I hate being reminded of that horrible day twenty years ago.

"That's old water under the bridge, Avery. Erin is over that incident, I'm sure." Mrs. Stevens turns her full attention back to me. "Not that I'm condoning what he did, dear. He was completely in the wrong, and you had every right to be upset and angry."

I don't really know how to reply. Am I over the incident? Nope. I still loath Jake Stevens. Before I have to reply, Maddox comes in the back door with a platter full of hamburgers and hotdogs. "Hey, Erin. It's good to see you," he says as he sets the platter on the counter in front of his fiancée. He gives her a quick kiss on the cheek. Avery's smile could blind a person, it's so big. You can feel the love and happiness radiating off of them. It makes me feel little tinges of jealousy, which just makes me feel like a horrible person. No one deserves to be happy more than Maddox and Avery. I've heard a few stories about their past and the love story that led up to today. They seem great together.

"Hi, Maddox. Thanks for including me in dinner tonight."

Maddox gives Avery a questioning look before she says, "Jake brought her." The smile never leaves her face.

"Really? Well, isn't that interesting. I better go see what ol' Jake is up to, shouldn't I?"

"He just brought me because he was helping with my sink," I defend but it's no use. He's already walking toward the living room with a smug smile on his face.

"Avery, why don't you call the guys all in here for dinner?" Mrs. Stevens turns to me as Avery leaves the room. "Sorry it's just burgers and dogs tonight. I usually make a large meal, but I didn't want Avery's new house trashed any more than it already is. Sometimes using the grill is the simplest way."

"No worries here. I love hamburgers."

Several guys start filing into the kitchen at that moment, so I take that opportunity to step away from the island, back and out of the way. I recognize Jake's dad, Michael, right away. He's much older and graying a little at the temples, but he still has the same, friendly demeanor he had when I was in seventh grade.

"You must be Erin. I'm Will, one of Jake's brothers—the middle child—actually." Will is almost as tall as Jake, but not nearly as broad. He has the same blue eyes, but he wears glasses. He has the bookworm look to him that I can relate to instantly.

"Hi, Will. It's nice to meet you."

"Likewise." We're joined quickly by another tall guy with the same blue eyes but light brown hair.

"I'm Travis, the youngest brother. Nice to meet you," he says as he extends his hand.

"Hello."

"And that one over there already digging into the food is Nate. You might remember him from school," Will throws in.

"Yeah, I think he was a year younger than me."

Just then my attention is drawn to the doorway when Jake and Maddox walk in. They're both tall with broad shoulders and radiate authority. Jake's eyes crash into mine and it feels like the room shifts. Why do I have this reaction to him? It's Jake Stevens for crying out loud. That's just it. It's Jake Stevens. Tall, toned, and devastatingly handsome. He's also the one person I despise the most.

I look away quickly as the rest of the family dives into the food set out on the island buffet-style. Avery is making a plate for Brooklyn, and Will and Travis are putting folding chairs up around the kitchen.

"Better get up there and make a plate before these guys grab all the food." I turn to face a very good-looking guy. He's not as tall as the Stevens boys or as broad. He has softer, gentler features, and he's honestly pretty hot. "Hi. I'm James."

"I'm Erin. Nice to meet you." So this is James, huh? Not bad.

The problem is, even though he rates pretty high on the hot-o-meter, I don't feel any reaction to him. Not to the feel of his eyes on my body. Not to the feel of his hand holding mine as we shake hands. Nothing.

"You too. I hear you had some troubles with your sink. Did you get it fixed?"

Before I can answer, I sense a presence approach behind me. My entire body is hyper-aware of Jake's presence. It's like my Spidey-sense goes off and things start to tingle. "She's all set. I helped her out and took care of it." Jake's tone is a little clipped with a no-nonsense edge to it.

James smiles at me, then at Jake. "Well, I'm glad she's all fixed up. If you ever need help again, you are welcome to call me. I'm just down the road from you."

"She'll be fine, James. I got it." Well, now he's just pissing me off.

"I can answer for myself, Jake." I turn to James and give him a friendly smile. "Thank you so much for the offer. It's nice to have someone close who can help if I should ever need it."

James looks back and forth between Jake and me, several times, before he laughs and gives me a little nod as he walks away to grab some food.

"Why did you do that?" I demand under my breath so we don't attract attention from his family.

"Do what?"

"Take charge of my life and make that decision for me. I might need his help someday. You don't get to make the choice of who helps me and who doesn't."

"Darlin', you don't want his help, trust me."

"Why not? He seems like a nice enough guy."

"Oh, he's nice enough. But he's just looking for something he can't have."

"And what is that?" I spit back at him.

"You." Jake never takes his eyes off of mine, burning straight through my corneas.

"And why can't he have me? I don't belong to anyone."

He leans in so that we're almost nose to nose. I can feel his breath against my lips and my tongue automatically darts out to wet them. "That's the thing, darlin'. You do belong to someone. You just don't realize it yet," he says, the corner of his lip turning upward in the cockiest, yet most delicious way. I swallow hard as he stands up straight and walks toward the food.

I have no idea why my body reacts the way it does to him. I'm just glad he doesn't know.

As I walk up behind him to grab a plate of food, he turns his full-watt smile on me. His eyes twinkle with mischief and knowledge. Okay, maybe he does know. Damn it.

The only two chairs left open are over by the dining room entryway so I head over and have a seat. I'm starting to chat with Travis when Jake comes and sits next to me. I can feel his leg pressed firmly against mine. I try to scoot over and limit the contact, but there's just no room to maneuver. Electricity shoots through my leg, straight to my lower stomach. Just one little touch from him has me practically panting and wanting to rub against him like a cat in heat. What the heck is wrong with me?

After dinner, Avery gives me a tour of their new home. It's definitely a great house, and I can hear the excitement in her voice as she shows me each room. My favorite part is the back patio. When Avery goes off to tend to Brooklyn, I slip outside for a moment to enjoy the perfect backyard space. Though it's January, freezing outside, and I don't have a coat on, I want to pull up a chair and start a fire in the big outdoor firepit.

"What are you doing out here?" Jake asks as I hear the click of the door latching shut behind him.

"Just enjoying this spot. It's stunning."

"It is stunning."

I turn around and look at him, but he's not looking at the firepit or the patio. He's looking at me. He never breaks eye contact as he walks up and stands a breath away. "I was talking about the patio."

"I know. I wasn't." Jake leans forward as if he's going to kiss me, but stops a mere whisper away from my mouth. "I want to kiss you so bad."

I close my eyes and don't say anything. Is that permission? He must think so because he leans in and ever so gently places his lips on mine. My mind goes completely blank at the contact of his lush lips on mine. Heat and energy thunder through my body as our lips touch for the first time. They're surprisingly soft and gentle as he slowly begins to move his lips over mine. I let out a sigh as I reach up and grab on to his shoulders. My knees feel weak and I start to sway where I stand. Jake wraps his arm around my back, pulling me against his hard body.

Just as Jake starts to deepen the kiss, the back door opens and we hear a throat clear. "Sorry to interrupt, but Brooklyn is looking for her uncle Jake before she goes to bed."

"Damn it," Jake mumbles under his breath. I pull away quickly and try my best to look unfazed by the interruption. Or maybe by the kiss. Oh, I don't know. Maddox chuckles as he walks back into the living room.

"We should go in. You don't have a coat on," Jake says as he places his hand on my lower back, guiding me toward the back door. "We'll finish this later."

"No, we won't. There will be no more of that. It shouldn't have happened."

"Oh, but it did happen, and I can't forget that now. I really, really enjoyed it. And I think *you* really did too," he says with another self-satisfying smile. I can't stop the blush that takes root in my neck and face. "I love your blush. It's kinda hot," he says as he pushes open the door.

"It's because it's cold outside," I retort with a lift of my chin.

He laughs, and says, "Sure it is. Twenty degrees outside and you're blushing because of the temperature. I think the only temperature you feel right now is *hot*." Jake all but whispers that last word, drawing it out and making it sound all sexy and dirty. Oh, who am I fooling, anyway? I am hot. Jake makes me feel that way. Being around him makes my temperature rise to feverish levels. I am so screwed—figuratively.

After Jake goes upstairs to help get Brooklyn to bed, I head into the kitchen. "Can I help you clean up in here?" I offer to Avery.

"Nope. I'm all done. You can stay and have a drink with me though. The guys are all upstairs trying to get a very excited three-year-old to lie down and go to sleep. They'll be up there for awhile," she answers with a laugh.

"Maddox seems like a great dad," I say before I can stop the words from spilling from my mouth. I recall hearing that Maddox isn't Brooklyn's real father, so why I said that, I'm not sure.

"He's the best. We want to get married quickly so he can adopt her as soon as possible. He's everything I've always wanted in a father for her. He'll be just as great with his own," she says with a distant look in her eyes.

"Oh...are you...are you pregnant?"

She laughs. "No. I'm just thinking out loud. I can't help it sometimes." She gives me a sheepish grin. "So, you and Jake, huh?"

"No. There is no me and Jake."

"So that wasn't you kissing him on my back patio just a little bit ago?" she smarts back with another big grin on her face.

"Oh my gosh, you saw that?" I throw my forehead down on my folded arms on the island top.

"Honey, everybody saw that. We sent Maddox out there to break it up before it went from PG-13 to rated R, and we'd have to turn on the sprinklers."

"I am so embarrassed. I can't believe I just made out with him in front of his entire family!"

Avery laughs again. "It's okay. Actually, it's really nice to see him kiss someone he didn't meet at Jack's."

"Jack's? The pub?"

"Yeah, sorry. Jake doesn't exactly do long term or commitment. He just seems to want to play for a little bit. Not that he won't change for the right girl or anything. Heck, Maddox was the same way before we started seeing each other."

I don't really know what to say to that. Is Jake just interested in hooking up with me just for the sake of hooking up? Before I can ask Avery any further questions, the guys all come down the stairs and descend upon the kitchen.

"Where's Maddox?" Avery asks her brothers.

"Trying to bribe Bean into going to sleep," Will says.

"We've read six books so far and still nothing," Travis adds.

"Well, it's because you were all up there at the same time. She was too excited to sleep," Avery replies. "I better go up and check on them."

"No, don't. Maddox was actually making headway with her," Jake adds. He turns to me sitting at the bar. "You ready to head out?"

"Yes." I stand up and we make our way to the front door. Jake holds up my coat for me in a very gentlemanly manner. But I can't help but wonder if he's just doing it to score.

I turn my attention back to Avery. She leans in to give me a hug. As an only child, I've obviously never had a sister. But if I did, I imagine goodbyes to go something like our exchange. A warm hug and maybe a peck on the cheek. "I'm so glad you could come tonight. Don't let Jake scare you off again," she says in a low voice.

"Thank you for having me. You have a lovely home."

I turn my attention back to the guys all gathering around. Nate leans in and gives me a big hug too. "Good to see you again, Erin."

"Hey, keep your hands to yourself," Jake growls behind me.

"I was just saying goodbye," he replies with a cocky smile.

"Next time, try a handshake, douchebag."

Nate laughs at Jake and throws me a little wink as he turns away. Jake places his hand on the small of my back and leads me out the front door. Even through layers of clothes and a coat, I can feel the heat from his hand on my lower back. It sends lightning-like sensations straight through me. If someone were to hand me a light bulb, I'd probably make it glow from the amount of energy and electricity racing through my body right now.

We're both fairly quiet on the ride back to my place. I'm lost in my own thoughts of work, home improvement projects, and of course, Jake. I wish I knew what his agenda was. If seventh grade has taught me anything, it's that history has a way of repeating itself, and I shouldn't trust the sweet-talking, charming smile of Jake Stevens.

"So, why don't you have a boyfriend?" Jake asks, breaking into my thoughts.

"Who says I don't have one?"

"I'd say that kiss said you don't. No way would you kiss me like that if you had a boyfriend."

"I didn't kiss you. You kissed me," I fire back.

"Does it matter who kissed who? The point is, *you* enjoyed it whether I started it or you started it."

"Whatever. You just caught me off guard. Like I said before, it'll never happen again."

Jake takes his eyes off the road for just a moment. "Oh, it'll happen again." When he returns his attention back to the road, I take the opportunity to change the subject.

"So, why did you become a cop?"

"It seemed like a great fit. After I got out of the Marines, I craved the discipline and the toughness that came along with it. Plus, I like the idea of helping people and taking the perps off the streets. Rivers Edge doesn't have the high crime like the bigger cities do, but we still have enough that you need to make sure you lock your doors at night and be careful."

"That's very honorable. I'm sure you make a good cop."

"I try. What about you? Why a librarian?"

I stare out the passenger window as I consider his question. "I've always liked to read. When I was growing up and moving from place to place, books were my constant. I spend more time at libraries than any other place. There's just something magical about them."

"You sound very passionate about it. I'm glad you found your calling."

"Me too." Before the conversation can get too much heavier, Jake pulls into my driveway. As I start to open the passenger door, he tells me to "wait" and gets out and walks around to my side. As he opens the door, he extends a hand to help me down from his truck.

"Thank you for the ride," I say as I walk up my front steps.

"No problem. Thanks for coming with me."

"Well, thanks for fixing my sink. I really appreciate it."

"Give me your phone," Jake says as he holds out his hand.

"Why?" I ask, hands firmly planted on my hips.

"I want to program my number in it so you can call me if you have any more trouble."

"Can you ask or does everything have to be an order with you, Jake?"

He sighs and his frustration is evident. "Erin, can I *please* see your phone so I can program my number in it? I would like you to have it in case you have any more troubles like the sink. *Please.*" He has so much sugar in his voice, I practically have a toothache.

"That wasn't so hard, now was it?" I ask as I dig in my purse and pull out my phone.

"You are the most difficult woman I know," he mumbles as he types his name and number into my phone.

"What are you doing now?" I ask as I see him continue to type long after what it would have taken to put in his name.

"I'm sending myself a text so I have your number. See?" He reaches out and displays my screen so I can see the text message.

Jake: I can't stop thinking about you and wanting your hot body, Erin.

"Nice. Very mature, Jake," I say with a roll of my eyes as I turn to head toward my door.

As I start to walk through my door, Jake grabs my arm and turns me around. "Wait. Don't you want to kiss me goodnight?"

"Seriously?"

"I don't want you to cry yourself to sleep tonight because you didn't get one."

"You are impossible."

"I prefer fabulous."

"I prefer infuriating."

Jake chuckles as he leans toward me. I can smell him. It's a heady mix of aftershave and soap. If I were a weaker person, I would lean in and lick his neck. I almost do it.

He kisses me on the corner of the mouth lightly, as if testing the waters. When I don't pull back, he brings his full lips to kiss me square on the mouth. His tongue slides along the seam of my lips, causing me to gasp and open my mouth. Jake's tongue dives into my mouth, kissing me like he's a dying man and I am the only thing keeping him alive. His tongue duels my tongue, sliding against each other in the most delicious way. My entire body goes up in flames.

I've never had a kiss like this one before in my entire life. I always thought kisses from past boyfriends were great, but compared to this kiss—to Jake's kiss—they were nothing if not completely lacking. Jake is exciting and intoxicating and I want more.

I lean forward and plaster myself against him. He's hard and firm in all the right places—and I do mean the right places. A moan escapes as I slide my body up and down against him like a cat.

"Darlin', we need to slow this down before I throw you over my shoulder and take you upstairs right now." His words come out in pants, his breathing hard, and I realize it mimics my own.

Reality sets back in and I pull back. "I can't believe I'm acting like this," I say breathlessly.

"If it makes you feel any better, I lose my fucking mind

whenever I'm around you too."

I grab a hold of what dignity and self-respect I can muster, and walk through the door. "Thanks again, Jake. I'll see you around."

"Yes, you will. Sweet dreams, Erin."

As I shut the door, my entire body seems to go limp. I slide down the door and sit on my entryway floor as I listen to Jake's truck start and back out of my driveway. What have I gotten myself into?

Chapter 5

Jake

I'm hanging the last of the beer signs in the man cave at Maddox's place when he comes over with a cold one from the beer fridge.

"This place is so damn sweet, man."

"Isn't it? This room is one of the major reasons I wanted it. Well, that and more space for Brooklyn to run around. I can't wait until the weather warms up so we can try out the backyard."

Maddox and I are both standing in the middle of the room, taking it all in. "We'll have plenty of barbecues back there."

"So, while I have you here, I have something I need to discuss with you." Maddox's tone turns serious and no-nonsense.

"What's up?"

"Avery and I have been talking a lot these past few days about getting married. I think we want to do it sooner rather than later. I want to adopt Brooklyn as soon as we're married."

"That's awesome, man."

"Well, it looks like we might be getting married on March first."

"Really? As in *this* March? Wow, that's great...and soon."

"Yeah, I want to get the adoption ball rolling the Monday

after the wedding. We've already met with the attorney who will handle the process. The problem is, Avery actually put Drake's name on the birth certificate so we have to go through the process of posting it and giving him a chance to respond. It pisses me off that he could have any say or input in this."

"I should have just killed him and buried his body in the woods when I had the chance," I reply, my body tense and filled with anger. Drake Connor doesn't deserve to have any say in this matter. He lost that right the day he abandoned my pregnant sister.

"I agree with you completely. That brings us back to the wedding. I need a best man. You interested?"

I'm humbled by the thought of standing next to my best friend as he gets married to my little sister. "I'd be honored, man." Maddox slaps my shoulder in a gesture of appreciation.

"Thanks. I couldn't imagine doing it without you next to me."

My best friend's words hit me right in the chest and it's hard to swallow over the lump in my throat. "You know back when I found out you and Avery were dating behind my back? I said you didn't deserve her. I've never been more wrong about something before in my life."

"You weren't wrong, Jake. I didn't deserve her. Frankly, she's the best person I've ever met, and I had some growing up to do. Even though I may not deserve her, no one will love her the way I do. She makes me want to be the man who does deserve her. She is my heart and my life; her and Brooklyn."

Without even thinking, I step in and give my best friend a hug. Not that tough-slap-your-hand-on-the-back kind of hug, but a full-blown hug.

"You're a good man, Maddox Jackson. Make my sister happy and shit." We both laugh as we step out of the embrace. "So does that mean I get to plan a kick-ass bachelor party?" I ask with a huge smile on my face.

"Of course, but no strippers. I don't want to piss off Avery."

"Ohhhhhh, my friend, there *will* be strippers!"

"I'll remember this for when it's your turn," he throws back at me with a laugh.

"Well, you'll be waiting for a long time because I'm never getting married."

"You say that now. Just wait. It'll happen."

My mind instantly fills with images of Erin. If I ever decided to settle down, I could entertain the idea of settling down with her. Good thing that'll never happen for me. Though, the thought of Erin settling down with someone else doesn't sit well either. It actually kind of pisses me off.

Where is this jealousy coming from? I've never been jealous of anyone. If a woman I'm with wants to flirt and talk with someone else, let her. There's another one just like her waiting in the wings. But the thought of Erin touching, laughing with, or marrying another man sends me into a funk I've never experienced before.

"Wow, what just happened there? You just had the weirdest look come over your face and now you look like you could punch a puppy," Maddox asks as he takes another pull of his beer.

"Nothing," I say as I take another big drink of my beer.

"Whatever. Something just happened. If I had to guess, I'd say it had something to do with a hot little redhead?"

"Shut up. I wasn't even thinking about her," I deny as I walk over to the fridge to get another beer.

"It's okay if you were. I'm just giving you a hard time. I do believe you deserve a little harassment back after the hell you gave me over Avery."

"You deserved all of that. I deserve nothing. There's nothing going on," I say as I turn back around to face him.

"I might actually believe that if I didn't bear witness to the kiss in my backyard. I thought I was going to have to turn on the sprinklers to cool you both down," he mouths off with a chuckle.

We stand there for a few moments doing the stare-down, both of us knowing I'm completely full of shit. "Fine. I like her. End of story."

"If you say so. I'll let it go for now, but I have a feeling we'll be talking about Miss Erin Anderson a bunch more in the future. Come on, let's go see if my daughter's up from her nap so we can hang those bookshelves in her room." With that, we walk out of the man cave and head in the house.

It's been two weeks since Erin and I shared that unforgettable kiss in her doorway. I've been doing everything I can think of to get her out of my head. I might be able to buy her I'm-not-interested-in-you bit if it weren't for the intensity of that kiss. So, I've decided to go to Jack's on this particular Saturday night and maybe take someone home with me. Nothing helps get your mind off your troubles more than mindless no-strings-attached sex.

Gabe's manning the bar when I get there and order a beer. James and a few other guys are already here and back by the pool tables, so I head toward the back to hang out for a bit.

"Hey, man. What's up?" James asks.

"Not too much. How's it going?"

"Good. Is Maddox coming up?"

"I sent him a text, but I doubt it. He won't take his balls out of Avery's purse long enough to come up here," I reply, which makes James and Collin laugh.

"You guys up for some pool?" I ask as I head to the pool table to rack the balls.

"You bet," James says.

After a couple of games, James catches my attention. "Dude, check out the hotties who just walked in."

I look up toward the door and notice four very pretty girls walk in and stroll up to the bar. The four girls order their fancy, fruity drinks and turn to survey the Saturday night crowd. When they see our small group in back, they start to make their way toward us.

"Evening, ladies. How's it going tonight?" I ask. They all reply in their best, flirty voice. The brunette in back walks up to me. She's definitely a looker. She has straight long brown hair, brown eyes, and legs a mile long. She's tall and lean, and her chest is practically spilling out of her top. All things I love in a woman.

"I'm Lauren. What's your name?" she purrs at me with a sexy look in her eyes.

"Jake."

"Well, Jake. Do you have plans this evening?"

"Nope."

"What do you say we head out and get to know each other somewhere else a little more private?" Lauren is batting her long— and probably fake—eyelashes at me as I reach for my coat. This is just what I need to get my mind off of a certain redhead.

"Absolutely." I turn back toward James, who is in the thick of his own babe-heaven, and throw him a wave. As I guide Lauren through the crowd toward the door, I can't help the extra spring in my step. This is exactly what I need.

Stepping out into the cold air on the street, Lauren links her arm in my own. The feeling of a woman touching me, rubbing up against me like a cat, used to make me hornier than hell. Knowing we are leaving to go have hot, and hopefully very sweaty, sex used to be a huge turn-on. But right now, I have this feeling I can't describe come over me. Now that she's touching me, I don't really want her to.

As we approach my truck, I start to slow down like my feet now weigh a hundred pounds each. I'm practically shuffling along, feeling weighed down by my own traitorous body. Lauren stands outside of my truck, waiting for me to open the door. I want to open the door, but my body has a mind of its own and won't do it.

"Are you ready?" Lauren purrs against my side.

"Uhh, yeah. Let's go," I say as I throw my passenger side door open. Lauren slides in but doesn't stop at the passenger seat. She slides right on over to the middle to ride "bitch."

As I walk around the front of the truck, I give myself a pep talk and try to pinpoint what the hell is going on with me. Lauren is beautiful with long legs, long hair, and is eager to jump into my bed for a one-night stand. And yet, I'm thinking of dozens of reasons why I should just take her back inside and head home. Alone. What the hell?

I climb in and throw the truck in gear. "Where to?" I ask as I get ready to pull out into the street.

"How about your place? I'm not close."

Do I want to take her to my house? Not really, but what other choice do I have? "Sure. Let's go."

The entire ride to my house, Lauren is rubbing my thigh with her long, bony fingers. Normally, I think fingers are sexy, especially as they grip a hold of certain parts of my body, but hers are just bony with long fake fingernails. She's babbling on about working out—or something—and I have a hard time focusing on what she's saying. All I can think about is what I'm about to do at my house. Since when is sex with a beautiful woman supposed to be torture? But that's what this feels like. Torture.

When we pull in, I find myself unable to get out of my truck. Lauren takes that as meaning the party is starting right here. She practically throws herself on my lap and starts kissing me, hands wandering up and down my chest.

I try to kiss her back, but it's just wrong. She doesn't taste right, and she's too aggressive as she slides her hand down to the crotch of my pants. I pull back and just look at her brown eyes.

"What's wrong?" she snaps.

"Nothing. I'm just not sure this is the best idea anymore."

"What? You don't think this is a good idea? My friends told me you were a sure thing. That you sleep with everyone. What the hell is wrong with me?"

"Nothing's wrong with you," I defend to the woman in front

of me on the verge of hysterics. You're just not the one I want to be kissing right now. "I'm just tired tonight from work."

"Whatever. You can take me back to my friends, now," she replies in a cold tone, scooting over to the passenger side of the truck. "I can't believe this," she mumbles as I back out of my driveway.

We're completely silent the entire trip back up to Jack's. Hell, I don't know what to say, and she's obviously pissed off at me. When I pull up in front, she doesn't say anything as she slams the door shut and stomps back inside.

Well, that went well. Smooth, Jake. Real smooth.

The first weekend in February, I can't take the radio silence with Erin any longer. It's Saturday and all I want to do is see her. My walls are starting to close in on me so I decide to go out for a drive. It hasn't snowed in several weeks so the roads are pretty clear and drivable. Maybe I'll head over to Avery and Maddox's place and hang out in the man cave.

As I'm driving through town, I notice a little red Bug sitting in the parking lot between the library and city hall. As if my hands have a mind of their own, they steer my truck into the parking lot. I park next to Erin's VW Bug and head inside the library.

When I pull open the door, I stop dead in my tracks at the sight before me. Erin is leaning over the counter handing a small child a book. The way her little body is spread out across the top of the counter like a buffet makes my pants tighten below the belt, as desire courses through me. I want to walk up behind her as she's spread across the counter and have my wicked way with her.

"Thank you for stopping in today, Caleb. Come see me again

soon," Erin says, pulling me out of my dirty fantasy.

I walk up to the counter and can't help but smile at the little boy grinning from ear to ear as he holds his new book.

"What are you doing here?" Erin asks with a look of surprise etched on her face.

"I was in the neighborhood and saw your car. I wanted to see how everything was going since it's been so long since I saw you last."

"Everything's fine. Thank you for checking. See you later," she says quickly as she turns back toward the stack of books sitting on the desk behind counter. I'm stunned by her reaction as I stare at her back. Did she just dismiss me? Erin gathers up the books and places them all on a cart and starts pushing the cart out from behind the counter. "Oh, you're still here." It wasn't really a question.

"Yep. What are you doing?"

"I'm going to put all these books away," she says as she pushes the cart toward the back of the library. I notice the library is empty and realize it's almost closing time.

"Want some help?"

"Umm, that's okay. I got it," she says, but I continue to follow her. I watch the gentle sway of her small hips behind her long skirt. It's definitely not a sexy outfit by any means, but she makes it look pretty good. I want to rip the skirt up over her hips and explore what's underneath.

She reaches the last row and starts searching the shelves. After finding the correct spot, she places the book back on the shelf. "I haven't been here in ages," I say, hands in my front pockets, casually leaning against the shelves.

"I'm surprised you've been here at all," she says as she goes about searching for the next book's proper place on the shelf.

"What is that supposed to mean?" I'm instantly on guard, standing up straight.

"It means just that. I'm surprised you know what the inside of the library looks like."

"I've been to the library before."

She turns and faces me, eyebrow raised slightly. "To read?"

"Baseball."

"Baseball? What the heck does that mean?"

I can't help the cocky smile that spreads across my face as my eyes twinkle with mischief. I relax my stance slightly, leaning back against the bookshelf. "I wasn't so much into the books here as I was with rounding the bases." Erin's mouth drops open and the shock is evident on her beautiful face. I walk up to her, looking down into her eyes, and lean forward until we're a breath apart. "Back here, in the back row. First, second, and even third base."

She gasps as her eyes become wide with shock. "You did *not* do that here! That's disgusting! What if someone caught you?"

"That's what makes it so thrilling, darlin'. You've never done anything sexual in a public place before? Somewhere where someone, anyone, can see you at any moment?"

"Never."

"Well, darlin', you are definitely missing out." Erin turns her attention back to the books on the cart and grabs the last few. Her hands have a slight tremor to them, and it's evident as she holds the books close to her chest.

I walk around the cart and stand right next to her. I can hear her breath coming out in a slight pant. She's definitely affected by me and what I'm saying. I love it when she gets all worked up and flustered. I can't help myself. "Do you want to know something I've never done in the library before?"

"You mean besides read a book?"

I lean in over her shoulder so my mouth is barely touching her ear. That little contact—the only contact I've had with her in almost a month—sends lightning straight to my pants. I'm half hard just from the slightest touch of my lips to her ear. I want more. "I've never hit a homerun in the library before," I whisper.

Erin drops the books she's holding and spins to face me. I grab her little face in my big hands and crash my lips into hers. She tastes like heaven. She immediately responds and opens her mouth for me. As my tongue plunges into the recesses of her mouth, she grabs on to my forearms and lets out a little moan. That noise is the greatest fucking noise ever. I want to hear how she sounds when I'm buried deep inside her.

The sound of the front door opening and slamming closed breaks into the trance we are in. She immediately pulls back, eyes as big as hubcaps, and touches her lips. Erin takes a few steps back until she's out of my reach and runs out of the aisle, heading toward the front of the library.

I go ahead and take a few moments to collect my thoughts—well, tame my hard-on is more like it—and pick up the dropped books before I head toward the front of the library. Erin's at the desk checking back in a few books brought in by a couple of kids and their mom, so I hang back by the magazine rack and wait until they're finished.

"Have a nice day," I hear Erin tell the group as they go out the door. I turn and head toward the counter, where Erin is clearly still flustered. She's nervously shifting her weight back and forth and is making herself look very busy by rearranging things on the top of the counter. She also won't make eye contact with me.

"I should probably head out," I say, deciding to take pity on her.

"Okay. It was good to see you. Have a great day," she says quickly with too much forced happiness.

"Erin." I pause and wait until she looks up at me. When her green eyes find mine, what I see in her eyes almost stops my heart. Lust. Desire. "Have dinner with me tonight."

She stares at me for a few moments, and I think she's going to ignore my question altogether. "Is that a question or a demand?"

"Both. Will you have dinner with me tonight?"

She hesitates, and I can practically see the wheels turning inside of her head. She wants to, I can tell, but something is holding her back.

"Why?" she asks quietly. So quietly, in fact, I almost miss the question.

"Why what? Why do I want to go out with you?"

"Yes," she whispers.

Because I want to spend time with you. Because I can't stop thinking about you. Because I want to finish that kiss we started in the dark back corner of the library. Take your pick. "I thought it would be nice to spend the evening with you and getting to know you."

She still stares at me with a weird look on her face. It's part confusion, part perplexed, part curiosity. I honestly have no idea how she's going to reply.

"What do you have in mind?" she timidly asks.

"I haven't really gotten that far yet. I didn't think you'd say yes."

"I haven't. I was just wondering what you were planning."

Oh, I can come up with a few things, but of course, I can't tell her that. "Dinner. Wherever you want to go."

"Just dinner?"

"Yes, just dinner." I lean forward, resting my elbows on the counter. "Unless you have something else in mind for afterward," I tease, eyebrows arched up in a suggestive manner. I can't hide the big smile on my face.

"No! Just dinner."

I straighten up. "Well, dinner it is. I'll pick you up at six," I say as I start to turn toward the door.

"I can meet you at the restaurant. You don't need to pick me up."

"I'll be there at six, darlin'," I throw over my shoulder just before I step outside, a big smile spread wide across my face.

Chapter 6

Erin

I think I'm having an out-of-body experience. I can see myself standing in front of the mirror in my bedroom, but I can't seem to move my body. I can only stare. Who is this person staring back at me? I used to think I knew her.

That person would *not* be wearing tight jeans and a very formfitting black sweater. That person would *not* have applied makeup—more than just a light dusting of eye shadow and mascara—all over her face. That person would *not* have accepted a dinner date with Jake freaking Stevens! He is the bane of my existence. The thorn in my paw. The rainstorm on my parade.

This person staring back at me is someone I've never met before. She's dressed up in trendy clothes. She's wearing makeup. She's watching the clock and waiting for Jake to pick her up. When did I become this person?

Before I can dive further into this dramatic turn of events in the life of Erin Anderson, my doorbell rings, signaling the arrival of my date. My date, aka Jake Stevens. I grab my small purse from my bed and head out of the room and down the stairs.

When I open the front door, I'm struck stupid at the sight of Jake in my doorway. He's wearing dark jeans that hug his incredible legs and hips, a dark-gray, tight-ribbed Henley shirt that shows off his broad, sculpted chest, worn boots, and a worn brown leather jacket. He looks delicious and I can't seem to process words.

"See something you like?" he asks with that big, cocky grin on his face. My face burns with the worst blush ever as I quickly turn away, realizing I was just busted ogling his chest.

"No. I was…" I stutter but can't even come up with a good lie.

"Darlin', you can look at me all you want," he says with a chuckle.

"I'm ready to go," I reply, quickly changing the subject and making a grab for my warm black peacoat.

Jake grabs a hold of my coat and holds it open for me. He can actually be a gentleman when he's not being a pompous, arrogant jerk. Jake places his hand on my lower back as we walk out the front door toward his old pickup truck. I can feel his hand burn me through my clothes, sending shivers of delight coursing through my entire body.

"Cold?" he asks. "We'll be inside in a second and I'll crank up the heat." If he only knew that the heat was already cranked.

Once we're backing out of the driveway, he turns his attention on me. "So, what do you feel like eating for dinner?"

"I'm not picky. You choose."

"Well, I was thinking about Laverne's Steakhouse. Is that okay?"

"That sounds great. I haven't been there since I've been back in town. Do Laverne and George still own it?"

"They retired a few years back, and their granddaughter, Lizzy, runs it now. She was a few years younger than us in school. Her brother, Pete, was our age."

"That's right. I remember him."

"So, how was the last half hour at the library before closing? Did you get all your books put away?"

I feel the blush creep up my neck as I recall the reason I was running behind on my end-of-the-day tasks. "It went fine once I was able to actually focus on getting my work done without any distractions."

"Is that what I am? A distraction?" he asks with a little grin on his face.

"Today you were. You came in there with the sole purpose of distracting me from completing my work."

"No, I went in there with the sole purpose of saying hello. The distracting just sort of happened."

"Well, it can't happen again. You can't come in there and try to round the bases in the back of the library, just because you feel the need. It's a professional, family friendly place and anyone could have walked up on us."

"First off, there was no one there and the ones who came in, we heard right away. And second, when I feel the need to round the bases in the back of the library, I guarantee, *you* will be begging me for that homerun, darlin'."

I have to restrain from fanning myself from the incredible heat permeating from the inside of the truck. No one has ever talked to me the way Jake does. It's controlling and edgy and sexy as hell. And I think I like it. I just can't let him know that. "Whatever. Just make sure if you come back to the library, you're there to check out books."

"Deal."

When we pull into the parking lot, I see it's just as busy as it used to be on Saturday nights. There are probably tons of locals in there, ready to drop a title onto whatever this night is between Jake and me. Is it an official date? I mean, it's just dinner amongst old classmates.

"What's wrong? You just got this funny look on your face."

"Nothing."

"Tell me," he demands without moving from the truck.

"I was just noticing that it's pretty busy and thinking that maybe we should go somewhere else less crowded."

"This place is always busy. You don't want to be seen with me? Somewhere so public where someone could start to ask questions?"

What the hell? Is he a freaking mind reader? "No. I just assumed we'd have a long wait."

Jake turns in the seat, grabbing my hand in his much larger one. "Listen to me, darlin'. Don't lie to me or beat around the bush. When I ask what's on your mind, I want to know. If you're worried about what everyone is going to think, then say that. We can go somewhere else, but promise me that you'll be one-hundred-percent straight with me all the time, even if it's something you think I don't want to hear."

I realize he's right. Trying to sugarcoat everything is one of my many flaws as a person. I've always been the people pleaser, the peacemaker. "Okay. I promise." I take a deep breath and look in his crystal-blue eyes. "Let's go inside."

"Are you sure?"

"Yes. I can handle whatever this town has to throw at me." Jake gives me a lopsided grin as he brings my hand that he's still holding up to his lips. He places a featherlight kiss on the outside of my hand.

"That's my girl," Jake says as he gets out of his truck and walks around to open my door.

"One more thing, I am *not* your girl," I throw over my shoulder as we walk toward the front door of the restaurant.

When we step inside, I am pleasantly surprised there isn't too much of a crowd waiting for seats. I walk toward the hostess stand with Jake right behind me. The girl looks up at me with a smile on her face. Then she seems to notice Jake and instantly frowns. "Jake Stevens," she says with disdain dripping from those two little words.

"Hello, Lauren. We'd like a table for two, please."

"Huh. Are you going to get cold feet halfway through the dinner and bail on her too?"

"Lauren," Jake says with a look that means business. If he was interrogating me right now, I'd probably confess all my secrets just based off of that one look.

"Jake," she spits back at him, narrowing her eyes into tiny slits.

I can't believe the conversation I'm bearing witness to. To Jake's credit, he's trying to not make a scene, but Lauren does not seem to have the same self-control.

"Hi. Obviously, you two know each other and that's great and all, but I'm wondering how long of a wait it is for a table?" I ask the hostess, trying to redirect her attention.

She sighs dramatically as she turns her attention back on me. "It'll be about ten to fifteen minutes."

"Great. I guess you already know what name to put down on the table. Thanks."

"Good luck, honey. He ain't even worth a fraction of the rumors you heard about him," she says as she turns to seat a couple in front of us.

I turn toward Jake, whose jaw is tight with tension. "What rumors?" I ask in a whisper.

"I'm assuming she's talking about the 'easy, only looking for a one-night stand' rumors."

"You were looking for more from her?"

"No. She was looking for the one-night stand. I wasn't interested. Apparently, she's still a little upset."

"Apparently."

We make small talk until our name is called—rather rudely if you ask me—and we're shown to our table. Laverne's Steakhouse has been a staple in Rivers Edge since it opened almost thirty years ago. Besides their signature steaks, they offer a wide selection of entrees including chicken, fish, and pork. Plus, their cheddar rolls are to die for!

I shuck my coat as I slide into the booth, cautious to not get myself tangled up in it. A few moments later, our server arrives with menus and glasses of ice water.

"My name is Chris. What can I get you folks to drink tonight?" she asks, pen ready to write our drink orders on her pad of paper.

"I'll have a light beer. Whatever you have on draft is fine."

"Same," Jake replies.

"Appetizer?"

"Yeah, do the variety platter, please," Jake tells Chris.

"I'll be right back with your drinks and to take your orders," Chris says as she turns to walk away.

"Light beer?" he asks with a raised eyebrow.

"What? Doesn't everyone like beer?"

"No. No, they don't. I don't think I've ever been with someone who hasn't ordered a big fruity drink."

"Well, then maybe you're hanging out with the wrong kind of people," I say with a pointed look.

"Maybe," he says with a small smile on his face. "So what looks good to you?" he asks as he redirects his attention back to the menu.

"Oh, you don't come to Laverne's Steakhouse and order anything other than the steak."

Jake looks up and just stares at me. I start to feel a little self-conscious about my appearance. Maybe I have something on my face? "What?" I finally ask when I can't take it any longer.

"Nothing. It's just that you haven't been here in twenty years."

"True. But twenty years ago, I used to come here with my parents at least once every few weeks, and I remember their steak was the only thing on the menu worth getting. Don't get me wrong, everything else that I've tried was good, but their steak was out of this world. I've never forgotten that."

"It's still that good. I came here a few weeks back with my family to celebrate Avery and Maddox's engagement."

"How did those two get together anyway? There's a bit of an age difference, isn't there?"

Chris delivers our beers at that moment. "What can I get you guys?"

"I'd like the signature steak with mushrooms and onions, medium. Twice-baked potato and steamed vegetables, please."

"I'll have the exact same," Jake adds.

After Chris leaves us with a basket of the delicious cheddar rolls that I've been fantasizing about for the past twenty minutes, Jake dives back into his story. "There is definitely an age difference between them. She's ten years younger than us. They started sneaking around behind my back last fall."

I about choke on my beer I was just starting to sip. "They were sneaking around?"

"Completely behind my back. I almost killed him. Smashed my fist into his face a few times too."

"Wow. Didn't see that one coming."

"Yeah, me neither. But I guess when I really look at it, they're great together. He treats her and her daughter like the princesses they are, and that's all I've ever wanted for my sister."

"That's great."

"Yeah, he's a great guy. He's adopting Bean as soon as they're married."

"When's the wedding?" I ask in between bites of roll.

"March first."

"As in *this* March first?"

"Yep. What does that give us? Three, four weeks?"

"Wow. Quickie wedding."

"Yeah, but they have good reason. Avery's ex is a true douchebag and hasn't ever been a part of Brooklyn's life. Maddox is filling that daddy role and loves every minute of it. He asked me to be his best man a couple of weeks ago. I can't wait."

"That's wonderful that you both have managed to maintain a close friendship throughout your youth. He was always a nice kid in school."

"Unlike me, right?" he asks without looking up from his cheddar roll.

I have no idea how to answer him but know he wants an honest answer. "You always seemed nice to everyone else. But to me, you seemed mean and spiteful." It's hard to swallow over the lump in my throat.

"Well, that's probably somewhat accurate. Though, I wasn't as mean and spiteful as you think I was. I always liked to tease you and get a rise out of you. You've always had this incredibly sexy blush."

"I was in seventh grade," I say dryly.

"Okay, so it was cute back then. Now, it's sexy."

"So, you picked on me just to embarrass me?"

"Yep. Well, that and because—" Jake is cut off as our waitress arrives with our steaks.

"You were saying?"

"I enjoyed flirting with you."

"Don't try to butter me up, Jake."

"You know back in grade school when boys liked girls and so they picked on them?"

"Yes." Jake raises his eyebrow at me. "No way. I was short and bony. I had frizzy red hair and big horrible glasses. There's no way you actually liked me."

"You were cute."

"I was horrible. I don't believe you."

"Oh, believe it, darlin'. I did everything I could to get your attention that year. You were adorable and so genuine. Like now."

"I don't need you turning on the charm, Jake."

"You think I'm charming?" he asks with another huge smile.

"You know you are," I reply dryly as I cut my steak.

When I take a bite, it's like a rainbow of flavor bursting in my mouth. I moan as I slowly chew, savoring every bite of the tender choice cut of beef. After I'm done chewing, I look up and see Jake's eyes are wide and fixated on my mouth. It's hard to swallow the meat in my mouth with him watching me so intently.

"What?" I mumble with half a mouthful of food.

"Huh?" he asks, returning his eyes to mine.

I finally get the meat down my throat. "You were staring."

He looks back down at my lips and shakes his head slightly, like shaking off a thought or an image. Maybe I did have some effect on him after all.

Following dinner, when the plates are cleared and the check is paid, we sit at our booth visiting and catching up over another beer. It's surprisingly easy to talk to Jake. I love listening to him talk about his family. He's obviously very close to his parents and siblings. Nate seems to be the brother he's closest to, but that could be because they're so close in age. He also talks about his time in the military and his work as a cop. My favorite story was when he was a rookie his first year on the force and got the call about a drunk man wandering down Main Street. What they didn't tell him over the radio was that it was old Mr. Forrester. He was stumbling home from Jack's Pub. And he was naked.

"To this day, no one knows what happened to his clothes. He was wearing them when he left the pub and definitely was *not* wearing them when I pulled up to give him a ride home."

I laugh at the mental image Jake painted for me. "That's hilarious!"

"It is now. Then, not so much. I caught ribbings from all the guys for weeks, hell months, for that call. You about ready to go? It's getting pretty late."

I look down at my watch and see that it's after ten o'clock. How we just managed to sit and talk for over four hours is beyond me. "Yes. Thank you for dinner. Are you sure I can't pay for half of the bill?"

"You're welcome, and I've already told you no. I asked you to join me. No way are you paying. Come on, let's head out." Jake helps me back into my coat and places his hand comfortably on my lower back. I never knew that simple gesture could ignite my blood and soothe my soul all at the same time.

After the short three-block drive, Jake pulls into my driveway.

That's when I start to get a little nervous. Am I supposed to invite him in? Will he even want to come inside?

"I had a great time tonight. Thank you, again," I say.

"I did too. I'll walk you to your door." Jake climbs out of his truck and comes around to open my door.

As we're walking up the front steps, I try digging in my purse for my keys. My fingers are shaking a little. I have no idea if it's from the early February cold or from the mere nearness of Jake. He's so close I can smell his aftershave, his soap.

When my fingers fumble with the keys, Jake reaches inside my purse and pulls them out, placing them in the lock and turning. "There you go," he says with a small smile.

"Thank you," I whisper, the words all but sticking in my throat.

My eyes are glued to his, my breathing coming a little heavier in anticipation. Jake leans forward ever so slowly and places a gentle kiss on my lips. His lips are warm and soft, and all I want to do is reach out and grab him, pulling him closer against me. I start to move my lips against his, taking the kiss deeper. He returns the kiss with a fury. In three point five seconds, we're all hands and lips and tongues.

Just as quickly as the kiss starts, Jake pulls back and rests his forehead against mine. Our breath is mixed together, our hearts beating wildly in our chests. "You better head inside before you get too cold."

"Yeah," I respond. "Good night, Jake."

"Night, Erin," he says, hands in his pockets as he watches me go inside the house. As soon as the locks are engaged, he turns and walks down the stairs, gets inside his truck, and drives away.

I stand here at the window and watch him go, thinking about the kiss that just shook me to the core. What is it about Jake Stevens that leaves me mindless and breathless? I have no clue, but I know I should probably stay away from him. The problem—I don't think I can.

Chapter 7

Jake

It's raining like a cow pissing on a flat rock. What a shitty Monday. I had a great dinner with Erin on Saturday night, and then nothing. More radio silence. If I don't hear from her today, I'll reach out and text later tonight.

Maddox is driving the squad car as we cruise through town heading toward Mom's bakery for lunch. Avery is supposed to meet us there with sandwiches, and as I glance down at my watch, I realize we're already running a few minutes late. Hell, we'll probably still beat Avery there. That girl is *never* on time.

"So I hear Erin decided to take pity on you and have dinner with you Saturday night."

"How'd you hear that?"

"Avery. They've been talking a lot lately. Erin came over yesterday and helped with some of the wedding stuff."

"Really?" I ask, not able to mask the shock in my voice.

"Yeah," Maddox replies as he pulls into a parking space in front of the bakery. "You okay with that?"

"Why wouldn't I be?" I ask as I get out of the squad car. "She doesn't really have any friends here yet, so it's good that she's hanging out with someone."

"Someone as long as it's a girl and not a guy, right?"

"Why? What have you heard?" I ask as I stand straight up, bracing myself for whatever blow Maddox is about to throw at me.

"Nothing. I can just tell that this girl gets under your skin."

"I have no idea what is going on, dude. I can't stop thinking about her. I want to drive by her house all the damn time, just to see what she's up to, or maybe catch a glance of her through the window. I can't even take a chick home from the pub anymore because I feel like it would be cheating on Erin. What the hell?"

I look over into the smug, smiling face of my best friend. "You're falling for her," he says matter-of-factly.

"Bullshit."

"Save your breath, dude. The same thing happened to me with Avery. One minute your life is smooth sailing with tons of chicks, then the next thing you know you are only thinking of doing a certain one and you can't imagine not seeing her or touching her. Happens to the best of us."

"First off, don't ever talk about doing only one chick when that one chick is my sister. Second, you're wrong."

"About what?" he asks with a laugh as he opens the door of the bakery.

I choose to ignore the question and head toward the back table. Surprisingly, Avery's already there and setting sandwiches out on the table for all of us.

"Hey, Sis," I say as I press a kiss to her cheek.

"Hi." Avery practically ignores me and stands up to greet her fiancé. She throws her arms around him, kissing him passionately.

"Knock that shit off. You're in a public place," I growl.

She laughs against Maddox's lips and smiles widely at me.

"Oh, big brother. What am I going to do with you? Oh, that reminds me. You and Maddox need to go get fitted for your tuxes by the end of the week. I already picked them out. You just need to stop by the shop and have them measure you."

"Can do. We're off Friday." To Maddox I ask, "Wanna head to

St. Charles on Friday?"

"Sure. I'll have Brooklyn on Friday since Rosemary is out this week visiting some family, but we can head over as soon as I grab her from preschool."

"Cool. Just come by my place when you're ready." I dive into my sandwich and turn back toward Avery. "So, what's this I hear about you hanging out with Erin?"

"Is that a problem?" she asks as she nibbles on a potato chip.

"No. I'm glad she has someone to hang out with, I guess."

"She's going with us this weekend for our dress fittings."

The thought of Erin hanging out with my mom and sister and her friends should make me sweat. But, honestly, it doesn't. Since when does it not bother me for my personal life and family life to collide? How about never. "That's cool. I'm thinking of asking her to be my date for your wedding."

Avery's eyebrow shoots to the sky. "Really? I was going to invite her too."

"Well, don't. Let me ask first."

Avery smiles over at me as she answers, "Okay."

As we're wrapping up lunch, the radio on my shoulder comes to life. "Three-Ten-David, you copy?"

"Dispatch, go ahead," I say into my radio.

"Reports of an attempted mugging at twenty-four Main Street, in front of the library. Victim is a thirty-two-year-old female, condition unknown. Over."

Erin. I'm up and out of my seat and heading toward the door before I even process what is going on. I hear Maddox's heavy footfalls right behind me.

"Ten-four. Unit en route," Maddox says into his radio after I don't respond. I am usually cool and calm in most situations, but right now I realize I'm a hair away from totally losing my shit.

My feet are barely on the sidewalk before Maddox is running around to the driver's side and throwing on the light. "Go!" I tell him before the door is even closed.

My heart is pounding, my palms are sweating, and I'm on the verge of panic as we speed toward the library. Fortunately, we don't have too far to go and we're pulling in a couple of minutes later. I'm out of the car before Maddox even has it in park, running toward the other squad car and ambulance on the edge of the parking lot.

When I approach the ambulance, I see Will bent over Erin, who is sitting on the sidewalk. She looks up at me as I approach, her green eyes filled with fear and relief. I feel like I can finally take my first deep breath since receiving the call to respond.

Will is checking Erin's neck and head for injuries as I crouch down next to her. I can't control my shaky hands as they reach out and touch her face. "Are you all right?" I ask in a voice I barely recognize.

"I'm okay. Just a bump on the back of my head."

"What the hell happened?" I ask as I watch Will feel around the back of her head. He must touch the part that she hit because I see her wince in pain.

"I was coming out of the library to walk down to the bank and make the daily deposit. A kid came up behind me and tried to grab the money bag. When I wouldn't give it to him, he pushed me into the brick building and I hit my head."

"You wouldn't give him the money bag? What the hell, Erin? No amount of money is worth getting yourself killed over," I thunder at her. I can't control the rage I'm starting to feel at the thought of Erin being seriously hurt or killed by some stupid kid looking to score a few bucks.

"Well, excuse me if I wasn't just going to hand over the library's money to some kid, who is probably looking to score a hit or some alcohol," she fires back at me, irritation and anger marring her beautiful features.

"Kids, do you think we can hold off on the lovers' quarrel until after I finish my assessment? I'd like to move her off the cold concrete and into the back of the rig as soon as possible," Will says with a stern look.

"Yeah, sorry," I mumble to my brother. Erin is still shooting daggers at me and I decide to take a moment to step back and find out what's going on with the suspect.

I stand and head toward Maddox, who is already talking to the first responding unit. "What do you have?" I ask with authority and attitude. I can't help it.

"The suspect took off on foot down Main toward Walnut Street, heading east. The third unit is searching the area now for him."

"Why don't you guys head out too and help search? We'll stay here and follow the victim to the hospital and conduct the interview." Officer Neil stares back at me and I can tell he wants to question my decision to stay, but he doesn't press the issue.

"All right. We'll head out and help search." Neil and his partner head toward their squad car.

"That was smooth. You should have just whipped out your dick and peed on the ground around her to mark your territory."

"Fuck off. I'm not dealing with this shit well right now."

"Clearly, Captain Obvious," Maddox smarts off. "They're loading her into the ambulance. Let's head over there and see what's going on."

When I approach the ambulance, I see Will already in the back, hooking Erin up to a monitor. "Are you taking her in?"

"Yep. I think she needs to have the bump on her head checked out. We'll meet you there."

"I'm riding with you."

"No," Erin and Will both say at the exact same time. Of course, I completely ignore both of them as I step up in the back of the ambulance. I turn toward Maddox, who is already shutting the doors.

He throws me a quick, "Meet you there," as he shuts the last door.

I sit down on the bench across from Will as he finishes hooking up the monitor to Erin's chest. I try to contain my growl as I watch my brother paw all over Erin from under her shirt, but I'm not very successful.

"If you can't sit there and be quiet, I can have you removed," he says with a look that tells me to settle down. Now.

"Why don't you ride with Maddox, Jake? I'm fine except for a horrible headache. I don't want to fight with you or argue about why I did what I did. I just want to rest and try to relax and get rid of this headache," Erin says as she closes her eyes and lies back against the gurney. When she does, her face winces in pain, again, at having bumped the tender spot on the back of her head.

I lean forward and take her hand in mine. Her fingers are freezing cold from having been outside far too long, so I rub back and forth with my large paws, trying to warm them up. When that hand starts to feel warm again, I grab the other and repeat the process. Erin finally looks relaxed as she rests on the gurney with her eyes closed.

It doesn't take too long to get to the Emergency Department at Rivers Edge Health Center. I throw open the back doors and step aside as the staff comes out of the hospital to help escort the patient inside.

Maddox is next to me a moment later as Will starts reporting stats to the staff around him. They have Erin inside the hospital emergency room a few moments later.

"Put her in room four," one of the nurses says. "Sir, you're going to have to wait out here until we get her all checked out. You can come in for your interview as soon as the doctor is done with his evaluation."

"I'm her friend," I say quietly.

"Well, stay here, and I'll come out with an update as soon as I have one. Okay?"

"Fine," I mumble as the nurse heads into the room, shutting the heavy door behind her.

And so, the waiting begins. I pace back and forth, up and down the small hallway as Maddox gives a status update to dispatch.

Will walks up and slaps my shoulder. "She's going to be fine, man. Just a bump on the head, and they'll probably check her out and make sure she doesn't have a concussion before they send her home."

"I know she's gonna be fine. I just want to be in there with her."

Will's lip curls up on one side in a slight smile. "You'll see her shortly. Hang in there, man," he says as he turns and heads back out toward the waiting ambulance.

"So, dispatch says they caught the kid. They found him hiding in the tool shed on the back of Martha and Jep Cordell's property. Apparently, their dog wouldn't stop barking so they called the cops. Kid is nineteen and from St. Charles. They're talking to him now at the precinct."

"Well, at least they caught the little bastard. Thank God he didn't hurt her more than he did."

"Mr. Stevens, you can go back now. Miss Anderson is asking for you," the polite nurse says. I follow her back down the short hallway but hesitate when I reach her doorway. "Go ahead," she says politely with an encouraging nod.

I knock as I step through the door. "Hey, how are you feeling?" I ask as I approach her bed. She looks so small in the big hospital bed, but at least some of the color has returned to her face. They also have her in one of those one-size-fits-all blue hospital gowns. Even with the oversized gown, she looks breathtakingly beautiful.

"Okay. We're waiting on the CT scan to make sure everything is fine before they'll let me go. Did they catch the kid who did this?"

"Yeah," I say as I grab a hold of her hand and sit down in the chair next to her bed. "They caught him hiding inside a shed a few blocks away."

"Good." Erin closes her eyes for a few minutes, and I think maybe she's dozed off, but then she starts talking again. "Thank you for coming with me to the hospital. It was nice to have someone with me."

"No problem. I'm sorry I jumped your shit earlier. It just made me crazy to think you could have been seriously hurt over a few bucks." I stroke the soft skin on her palm with my much bigger, calloused fingers.

"Yeah, well I have to account for every penny I spend at the library, and I didn't want to lose any just so some kid could score a hit."

"I understand why you did it, but that doesn't mean I like it or it was a smart move."

"So what happens next? Do you have questions to ask me?" Erin asks with her eyes still closed.

"Yeah, Maddox and I have to conduct the interview. Are you up for a few questions?"

"Sure."

After Maddox joins us in the room and the questions have all been asked and answered, the radiology staff comes down to get Erin for her CT scan. Maddox and I return to the waiting area, but this time, I'm much calmer as I wait since I got to talk to Erin.

When she's returned to the ER, the doctor comes in and tells us the scan came back clear. She's ordered to take it easy for a few days and take Motrin for the headache.

Since I'm still on duty and in the squad car, I call my mom to come get Erin from the hospital and take her home, with the promise to stop by as soon as I'm off work.

"You don't have to do that. I'll be fine when I get home and can get some rest."

"I'll be there as soon as I'm off work," I reiterate, leaving no room for any more arguments from her. That earns me an eye roll of those beautiful green eyes.

When Mom pulls up to the ER entrance, I help Erin into the front seat of her car. I lean down and can't help but inhale the wonderful scent of her hair. It smells like something tropical, and I'd love to dive my hands into it again. Since I don't want to hurt her head further, I settle for a gentle kiss on the crown of her head.

"Thank you," she says with a shy smile.

"I'll see you later. Get some rest and I'll bring over some takeout for dinner."

"Okay," she says as Mom pulls out of the drive.

"Let's go, Romeo. We have paperwork to fill out at the station," Maddox says as he heads toward the squad car. Only a few more hours left of this shift and I can head over to Erin's and check on her, which I'm actually looking forward to. I want to see her and take care of her. I want to be there for her.

Wednesday brings my day to hang out with Bean. Maddox was called in to work to fill in for a sick officer, so I volunteered to watch my niece. It's hard to believe she's going to be four in just a couple of months.

After Avery drops her off with tons of dolls and toys, we set out to play in my living room. Even though I'm wearing a little plastic tiara and holding a little baby doll wrapped in a pink blanket, I wouldn't trade these moments with her for anything. Since Maddox and Avery got together, I actually watch her less than before since Maddox has her on our days off.

For lunch, we decide to head out and grab some takeout. My mind wanders to Erin, who is back to work today after having the last day and a half off following the mugging incident. I decide to send her a quick text to see if I can grab her lunch while I'm out.

> **Me:** Hungry? Bean and I are grabbing food. We can bring you some.

It takes her a few minutes to reply.

Erin: No thanks. I brought a sandwich.

Well, shit. I was hoping to grab a chance to swing by and see her. I guess I'll have to be a little more creative.

Me: OK. Have a good one.

Erin: Thanks. You too.

She's definitely not getting rid of me that easy. After Brooklyn and I hit the local fast food restaurant for lunch, I decide that maybe a trip to the library is in order. "Hey, Bean. Wanna go to the library?"

"Yay! Da wibwawy!"

I find the closest empty parking spot in the lot, grab my niece, and head into the library. The heavy door slams shut behind us as we walk toward the front counter. I can see an older lady over in a seating area reading. Otherwise, the place looks deserted. Where's my favorite librarian?

When I approach the counter, Bean walking next to me, I see Erin sitting at the desk in the office. I clear my throat as I rest my elbows on the counter and give her one of my signature killer smiles. The one that makes panties drop. I know this for a fact. This smile works wonders.

"I thought I told you not to come back unless you were checking out books," she says as she looks up over her cute dark-rimmed glasses. Erin mentioned at dinner that she doesn't normally wear glasses anymore since she had corrective vision surgery a few years back, so I'm assuming those are readers.

Instead of responding to her comment, I reach down and pick up Bean, setting her down on the counter.

"Oh," she says as she quickly gets up and walks around the desk toward the counter. "I didn't realize you had a guest with you. Hi, Brooklyn."

"Hi! I want to get books, pwease!"

Erin smiles down at Brooklyn's sweet face. "You want to get

some books? You got it! Come on, let's go." I set Brooklyn down on the floor as Erin comes around the counter to join us. Erin holds out her hand for Brooklyn, who takes it with no reservation. The sight of Erin and my niece walking toward the children's section makes my chest tight. My heart feels like it's slamming into my rib cage. It's the damnedest sight, but it doesn't scare me like it would have any other time. Any other woman. Erin walking with my niece, holding her hand, just seems right. It fits.

When they reach the children's section, Erin starts talking to Bean about what kind of books she likes. "Pwincess!"

"Well, you are in luck, little lady. I have a huge selection of princess books right over here." She guides Bean to a section on a short bookcase and starts to pull them off the shelf.

"Dis one!" she exclaims as she waves a book in front of Erin's face.

"*A Princess Like Me*. Oh, this one's a good one *and* it's a pop-up book. Come here," Erin says as she walks toward a large, worn, overstuffed chair. Erin sits down and places Bean on her lap. She flips open the book and starts to read.

My mouth goes dry and my lungs struggle to pull oxygen into them. I can't help but stare at the sight of them reading a book together. Brooklyn is snuggled into Erin's lap, listening intently as she reads the story. Erin uses different voices for each of the characters and has such a smooth, calming delivery. She's a natural, and I can see how much she loves her job in the way she reads to my niece.

One book turns into two, which turns into six. Brooklyn's eyes are closed and have been for the past several pages, but I don't interrupt Erin because I love listening to the sound of her voice.

When she gets to the end of the book, she looks down and realizes that Brooklyn is asleep. She looks up, her green eyes fixed on mine, and she smiles as she lays her head down on top of Brooklyn's. It's the most perfect moment. I want to stay right here, like this, forever.

Wait a minute! Back it up. Forever? Where in the hell did that come from?

I get up and take the book from her hand, returning it to its correct place on the shelf. As I bend down, intent on taking Brooklyn from her lap, my eyes seem to focus in on Erin's lush lips all on their own. I want to kiss them so fucking bad. I know we're in the middle of the library and she'll probably throw a fit, but I just can't seem to stop myself.

I lean forward and gently place my lips onto hers. She sighs against my lips and the sound sends all of my blood straight below my belt. I run my hand along her neck, taking in the gentle curve and soft skin. I know deepening the kiss is a bad idea, but I can't seem to remove my lips from her body. I place light kisses down her jaw to her neck. I lick her pulse point and can feel it beating rapidly underneath her tender skin.

I want to continue kissing her more than anything in the world, but I can't do it when she's holding my sleeping niece on her lap. So, I regrettably pull back a little to look at her beautiful face. Her eyes are still closed and her mouth is opened slightly, forming the cutest little 'o.'

"I should get her back to my place so she can finish her nap." I reach down and gently lift Brooklyn from Erin's lap and can't help but rub against her chest a little. Hey, I'm a guy. Her breasts are full and her nipples are hard little peaks. I'd give my right nut to be able to explore them right now.

But Uncle Duty calls, so I head toward the door with my sleeping niece cradled in my arms. Erin helps me get her coat onto her limp body, which is no easy task.

"So, I have to work all weekend, and the guys are all getting together at Maddox's man cave to plan the bachelor party Friday night, but I'd like to see you if I can. I know Saturday I get off a little late, but I want to stop by after I get off work at nine."

"Is that a question or a demand?" she asks with a little irritation in her voice.

I love how quickly she goes from zero to sixty. It makes me

wonder if she gets worked up in *other* ways just as fast. "Both. I won't stop by if you don't want me to."

"I should be back by then."

"Where are you going?" I ask as images of Erin out on a Saturday night with someone who isn't me flash through my mind.

"I'm going with your sister, Mom, Holly, and Maddox's mom to the dress fittings," she replies as she crosses her arms over her chest. The motion presses them together and up on display. I can't help but stare at the succulent view.

"My eyes are up here, Jake."

"I know they are. I wasn't looking at your beautiful eyes, Erin," I reply with a cocky grin.

"Obviously."

"I'll see you Saturday night," I say as I head out into the February air with Brooklyn tucked securely in my arms. Oh, yes. I have plans to see plenty of Miss Erin Anderson on Saturday night.

Chapter 8

Erin

I arrive at Avery's house at ten o'clock to meet up with everyone so we can head to her dress fitting. The wedding is in exactly two weeks, and there are still tons of final details to wrap up.

Avery tells us on the ride to St. Charles that the guys got fitted for their tuxes yesterday and planned Maddox's bachelor party last night. "It's going to be next Saturday. Same night as mine."

"What are you guys doing?" I ask.

"I won't tell her," Holly says with an ornery laugh. "Just be ready at six o'clock, Erin. You won't want to miss this one!"

"There better not be any strippers, Holly. I don't think I'm comfortable with that," Avery says as she looks at her mom who is driving.

"Oh, Avery. How often does a girl get to watch hot men strip down to a thong as you stuff dollar bills down their pants?" Mrs. Stevens asks with a big smile on her face.

"Mother!"

"Why do you think I told you I wanted to attend your bachelorette party so bad, and you had to find someone else to watch Brooklyn for the night? You think I want to miss that?"

Avery moans with a look of pain on her face. Holly and I can't help but laugh at the entire situation. I lean over and whisper under my breath so Avery, riding in the passenger seat, can't hear me. "Are there really going to be strippers?"

She whispers back, "Like I said. You won't want to miss this one."

When we arrive at the bridal boutique, Mrs. Jackson is waiting for us. The employees sweep Avery and Holly away to get them in their dresses. The two moms also head back to try on their mother's dresses for the wedding, so I wander around the rows and rows of beautiful wedding dresses. White chiffon, ivory lace, beads, and sequins; you name it, it's here in this huge room, just waiting for the bride to come pick that dress and declare it "perfect."

I'm drawn to a beautiful ivory gown hanging on the mannequin. It has a deep scoop neck, thin spaghetti straps, and a satin bodice with a small train that is breathtaking. It's so simple and elegant. It truly takes my breath away.

When I was a little girl, I never understood those girls who fantasized about their wedding day to Prince Charming, planning out every detail like it's happening tomorrow. No, I'd always much rather get lost in a book than a fantasy. Which, I guess if you look at it, that's what I did too through books, but somehow this just seems different.

As I touch the soft satiny material of this beautiful gown, I realize it's the first time I actually stop and consider what it would be like to get married. To have someone to come home to every night; to wake up next to every morning. Someone to fight with and love. I do want that. Desperately. I want the fairy tale like in the novels.

My phone chiming brings me out of my daydream. I pull it out of my purse and look at the screen.

Jake: What are you doing?

Instead of typing a reply, I snap a quick picture of the row of dozens of wedding dresses and hit send.

A few minutes later, he replies.

Jake: That's right. I forgot. Which one are you getting? *insert winky emoji*

His question makes me stop dead in my tracks. Does Jake think I'm here getting a dress? Or scouting out dresses for my future wedding?

I fire back my reply as quickly as my shaky fingers will type.

Me: None.

Jake: I like naked better too. Let's go with that. *insert smiling emoji*

I stare at my screen, not really knowing how to reply to him. A few moments later, he replies again.

Jake: Gotta traffic stop. See ya tonight.

I reply a quick *Bye* and drop my phone back in my purse like a hot potato. I can't stop looking at the beautiful ivory gown hanging on the mannequin. And now I'm thinking about Jake. Could I actually be considering a future with Jake? When we're not fighting with each other, we seem to enjoy our time together. But Jake will never settle down. His sister has told me that. Heck, *he* has told me that.

My thoughts are interrupted as Mrs. Stevens comes up behind me. "That's a beautiful dress, dear. With your complexion and hair coloring, you would look stunning in it."

"Oh," I say, startled when I realize I'm still holding the silky material of the gown in my hand. I drop it and turn to face Jake's mother. "I was just browsing the dresses while I wait for the bride to come out, Mrs. Stevens."

The friendly, warm woman smiles at me. "Elizabeth, please. You know, dear, Jake is a very stubborn boy. He was my most stubborn child, which I'm sure comes as no surprise to you. One of these days, he's going to realize the best things in life are right in front of you the whole time."

Is she talking about me? I furrow my brows in confusion. "Jake and I are just friends, Mrs—Elizabeth."

"Yes, you are. For now. But I saw the way he was looking at you, watching you when you came to Avery's for dinner the night they moved. Plus, I heard all about that kiss on the patio."

My face burns bright red. "Jake and I can barely stand to be in the same place together. We fight about everything."

"Sometimes, my dear, fighting with the one you love is better than not fighting at all. Fighting means you have passion and you're alive. Fighting symbolizes your desire and your lust. Fighting represents love." She gives me a warm, motherly smile; a smile that I haven't received from my own mother in so long. "Plus, the making up afterward makes the fights that much better," she adds with a wink as she turns and walks toward Avery, who is walking out in her beautiful wedding gown.

For the first time in my life, I wonder if Jake and I actually have a chance at making something work between us. Could I fall in love with Jake Stevens? I'm afraid that the answer is already a *yes*.

Jake pulls in after nine thirty. His golden-blond hair is still damp from the shower he must have taken before he came over. I notice it is spitting snow as I open the door for him.

"Come on. Grab your coat," he says when I open the door for him.

"Excuse me?"

"Let's go."

"Ummm, how about you *ask* me instead of demand it?"

He sighs dramatically as he rephrases his statement. "Erin, I have a little surprise for you. Will you please grab your coat and come with me for a little bit?"

"Yes," I say matter-of-factly, as I reach into the hall closet and grab a winter coat.

"Let's go. We don't have much time." Well, so much for polite and "asking."

"Where are we going?" I ask as I slide into his truck.

"The Ice Cream parlor opened today. I thought we'd go get an ice cream before they close for the night."

"But it's like thirty degrees outside. And it's snowing."

"I know," he replies and concentrates on getting us to the ice cream parlor before it closes at ten.

When we pull into the drive-thru, Jake asks "What do you want?" before rolling down his window.

"Hot fudge sundae, please."

When the young girl opens the window in her winter coat, Jake orders two hot fudge sundaes. I try to pull some money from my purse, but Jake holds up his hand. "I invited you to this surprise, I am paying."

"Thank you," I say as I take the first sundae handed to us through the window.

"You're welcome." Jake throws the truck in drive and heads out of town.

"Where are we going?"

"I thought we'd watch the snow fall at the river and enjoy our ice cream."

"Oh, the river. I haven't been there in twenty years. In fact, I don't think I've ever been there."

"You've never been to the river? How is that possible?"

"Well, when we arrived in Rivers Edge, I wasn't allowed to go anywhere by myself yet, until my parents felt a little more comfortable. Then, it turned cold fast. And I was gone in March, so I didn't get to enjoy the summer months at the river that everyone talked about."

Jake pulls into the long lane that runs parallel to the snow-

and-ice-covered Missouri River. This part of the river is much shallower and narrower than the majestic Missouri River. It's quiet and peaceful here.

Jake shuts off the truck as we dive into our sundaes. "So, can I ask you something?"

"I guess."

"Why did you leave so quickly in seventh grade?"

The question makes my heart stop beating. My mind wanders back to those last couple of humiliating days before I left Rivers Edge. I don't want to discuss this with him. I don't want him to know exactly how much he affected me all those years ago.

I shrug and scoop another spoonful of the cold dessert.

"Don't do that," he says with authority in his voice.

"Do what?"

"Don't act like it's nothing. I asked. I want to know. Remember our date? You promised me you'd tell me the truth when I ask you a question."

"I just don't think it's wise dredging up the past, Jake. It's done. Over."

"I want to hear your side of it. I want to hear it from you."

I sigh deeply and return my focus on my ice cream. I hate confrontation and the thought of having this conversation with Jake right now turns the ice cream in my stomach sour.

"Erin," he says softly with a little pleading in his voice.

"I just needed to get away, Jake. The thought that everyone at school knew my secrets, my thoughts, hurt me. I wanted to be invisible, and when you showed everyone my journal, you took that away from me. I was the girl who whined about her parents. The girl who cried herself to sleep at the thought of having to pick up and move one more time. The girl who had the biggest crush on the boy that every girl in school had a crush on. The girl who watched her entire life unravel before her eyes and couldn't do a thing to stop it." I stare straight out into the night sky. There are no lights out here, no traffic, no sound. Just Jake and me and the river.

"Why did you leave? Why didn't you stay in Rivers Edge with your parents?"

"Because the thought of seeing you every day was more than I could handle. I couldn't stand to look at you and pretend what you did didn't hurt and destroy me. That journal was all I had, Jake. It contained my thoughts and my dreams. I shared everything within those pages and you took it and shared it with everyone at school. I didn't want to see your face and be reminded of how you betrayed me."

Jake remains quiet but I can feel his eyes burn into the side of my face. I don't want to look at him, but curiosity eventually gets the better of me.

"Where did you go?" he asks, his voice small and ashamed.

"I went to Jackson, Mississippi to live with my grandma. It was actually for the best. My grandma was able to convince my parents to just let me stay there with her to finish out my school years. Finally, I had a home. A real home. I didn't have to move around anymore. I was finally happy. I met a group of friends that I actually got to spend more than a few months with before I had to leave. I graduated with friends. When I went to college, I was able to remain living with my grandma. I actually stayed with her until last year. I always planned to move into my own place, but my grandma just got weaker and weaker as the years went on. I was afraid to leave so I stayed. She died last spring. After that, I was ready to get out of Jackson and start my own roots somewhere else."

"Why Rivers Edge?"

"A classmate we went to school with reconnected with me a few years back on Facebook. In one of our many conversations, she mentioned Mrs. Masterson was planning on retiring and the city was going to search for a new librarian. I applied. They offered. I accepted."

Jake is quiet again for a few moments before he starts up his truck and drives back the way we came. I feel raw and emotional after our conversation, so the fact he's taking me back home is welcomed.

We don't speak the entire ride back to my place. I still hold the melted bowl of ice cream in my hand when he pulls into my driveway and parks behind my Bug. I have no idea what he's thinking. I'm sure he's just dying to get this crazy, overly emotional girl out of his truck.

"Well, thank you for the ice cream. I guess I'll see you around," I say as I turn toward the door to hop out.

"Wait," Jake says. The snow is coming down hard now, and I can barely see my front steps. "Please don't go." Jake's voice is raw with emotion. He sounds almost pained. I don't want to turn and see his face. I know if I do, I might actually believe whatever it is he is about to say. "Please look at me, Erin."

I take a deep breath and slowly turn around, steeling myself for the reaction I know is coming. When my eyes lock on his, I can't fight the tears that spring in my eyes. His eyes are so full of pain and hurt. It's too much. I need to get out of this truck.

"I need to go inside."

"Erin, I'm...I'm so fucking sorry for what I did back then. I have no excuse for why I did it. I was just a stupid kid who was trying to get a rise out of you; trying to get you to notice me."

"Notice you? Why would you want me to notice you?"

"I wasn't lying at dinner that night when I told you I was trying to get your attention. I liked you."

"So you humiliated me and embarrassed me? Why? So I'd like you? Do you have any idea how messed up that is, Jake?"

"I didn't say it was logical. I was a kid. A kid who was used to getting exactly what he wanted, when he wanted it. I went about it the wrong way. I'm sorry."

"Well, you're sorry. Great. Thank you." I turn and open my door. "I'm going inside. Thank you for the ice cream, again. Have a great life."

"Wait!" he yells as he whips open his truck door and meets me around the front of the truck.

"What, Jake? You've apologized. You don't have to be nice to me anymore just to make yourself feel less guilt. I forgive you. You're free." I blink rapidly in the falling snow. It's hitting and melting on my face, my hair, my coat.

"Is that why you think I've been nice to you? I've been hanging out with you because I've felt guilty for what happened twenty years ago?"

"Isn't it?" I quip.

"No!"

I turn to walk toward my house, but Jake grabs my arm and spins me back around. My body crashes into his like it's being slammed into a brick wall. He's a foot taller than me so my face basically hits him straight in the pecs. "I'm tired, Jake. I don't want to fight with you anymore."

"I don't want to fight with you either, Erin." Jake strokes his thumb up and down my numb cheeks. His fingers feel warm against the frostiness of my exposed skin.

"Then what do you want?" I ask, my eyes pleading with him. For what, I'm not sure.

"I want...I just want...you," he whispers the last word as his full lips descend onto mine.

When our lips lock, it's like an explosion of feelings. Heat spreads through my entire body. I feel slightly lightheaded, like I'm starving for oxygen. I feel desire and longing. And I can feel all the exact same reflected in Jake's kiss. He kisses me like he's starving and longing and scared all at the same time. This kiss says everything.

The February air is cold and the snow is wet, but I don't really feel it anymore. I'm lost in a different world, like I'm on the outside looking in. All I feel is Jake. His lips. His tongue. His body pressed hard against mine.

Jake's hands dive into my hair, holding my head as he devours my mouth with his own. I wrap my arms around his waist, pulling myself tightly against him. I feel all of the hardness of his body. His hard chest and stomach. His very large hard-on through his pants.

Knowing he wants this as much as I do, that I've brought him to this crazy, almost out of control place, is an intoxicating feeling. His back muscles jump as I snake my hands under his shirt to get a feel of his warm, bare skin. I want to touch him—I need to touch him—everywhere.

Jake pulls away from my swollen lips just long enough to ask the question I've been waiting to hear. "Can I come inside?"

"Yes," I whisper. But my body is anything but whispering. It's screaming and shouting at the top of its lungs, begging for him to go inside with me. Everything about him makes me want to scream.

Jake lets out the breath I didn't realize he was holding and kisses me one more time. Then he drops his hands from my hair and grabs my hand, pulling me up my walkway, up the stairs, and toward my front door. My hands shake as I pull my keys from my purse and slide them in the lock.

Once the door is open and we're inside the foyer, Jake spins me around and presses me against my closed door. His large frame is essentially holding me captive against the door and I couldn't care less. I want him to possess me, captivate me, consume me.

Jake runs his large hands down my back to my butt and lifts me up, bringing me face-to-face with him. I wrap my legs around his large body as he devours my lips again. There's a frenzy in the kiss, like we're both rushing to get to the finish line because going any slower might just kill us both. Our tongues are dueling, our lips sucking, our hands exploring.

"You're wearing entirely too much clothing, darlin'," Jake mumbles against my open lips. "And besides, as much as I want to, I'm not taking you against the wall right now."

"You're not?" I ask completely breathless and panting.

"Not for our first time," he says with that half smile I love. "Come on," Jake says as he removes my coat and then his and throws them on the bench by the front door. "I have big plans for you and me tonight."

"You do? And what might those be?" I ask, a shy smile

spreading across my face.

"I'm more of a 'show you' kinda guy, darlin'. Which way to your bedroom?"

Since I'm so breathless—and honestly, I'm not sure I could form more words at this moment anyway—I point up the stairs as indication of where we should be heading. Jake bends down and picks me up so I'm straddling his front, legs locked around his waist, arms tightly around his neck. I know he's plenty strong and should have no problem holding me up, but we have to go upstairs, and I don't want to wear him out.

Jake takes the steps two at a time, his long strides easily lifting both of us up the stairs. When we reach the top, he's not even winded. In fact, he seems more energized. He kisses me again with abandon, holding me tightly against his body. I can feel the heat through our clothes. I don't know if it's from him or me, but the temperature just skyrocketed considerably on the way up here.

It's like my body has a mind of its own. I grind my core against his stomach, trying to relieve the ache I feel between my legs. "You better not do that too much, darlin', or this party is going to be over before it really gets started," Jake growls against my lips.

I can't help it though. My body is screaming for release like I've never felt before. In fact, I've never felt anything like this before. The few times I've had sexual encounters in the past, well, they were nice, at best. The guys I've always dated were the types who were more concerned about their studies or careers. I always came a very distant second.

"Please, Jake," I say as I pry my lips off of his. "I need you."

"I'm not going anywhere, darlin'. Which room is yours?"

I point again and return my mouth to his. I can't get enough of his kisses. He's so possessive and domineering, even in his kiss. I want him to possess me. He is my drug. He is the key to my survival.

Jake walks into my room and gently sets me down on my bed, but doesn't join me. He stands over me, eyes blazing a hot trail down my body. I wiggle under his gaze, which causes him to moan.

Jake begins the painstakingly slow process of undressing me. He starts with my boots and socks. He's going so slow, staring so intently at me, it's like he's committing to memory every part of my body.

"Sit up," he commands. Jake has clearly taken control and I realize I want him to, need him to. He has so much more experience at seduction and foreplay than I do. I wouldn't even know how to seduce him.

Jake reaches down and ever so slowly lifts my sweater. He runs his fingers up my sides, burning my skin with his touch, as he guides my shirt up and over my head. I shiver at the feel of his hands roaming over my instantly goose-bumped skin.

He takes in my white cotton bra and groans, "I never knew white cotton could be so sexy." His lips are on mine a moment later. I honestly don't think white cotton is sexy in any way, but the way Jake is looking at me, making me feel, I feel like it's the sexiest thing in the world.

He continues to kiss me as his hands begin to wander down my neck toward my chest. My nipples are hard and aching to be touched. Jake palms one breast through my bra, kneading it with his big strong hands. He lightly pinches my hard peaks causing me to moan against his lips.

He trails kisses down my chin, my neck, making his way slowly toward my breasts. He gives the cotton a gentle tug, freeing my breasts from the restraints of the bra. His mouth descends upon them immediately. His mouth and tongue are hot and wet and send lightning through my body, straight to my core. The sensations cause me to writhe underneath him as I raise my body upward, seeking more contact with him.

Jake kisses his way down my stomach. He reaches down and releases the button on my jeans. With his large hands, he starts the process of removing my pants. I wiggle under his stare, his touch, and close my eyes at the intense sensations coursing through my body.

Jake's growl causes me to open my eyes. He's staring at my plain white cotton bikini underwear. "These are soaked. It's the hottest fucking thing ever." He dives down, placing soft open-mouthed kisses to my thighs. I feel his large fingers pull the cotton to the side, exposing my core. Goosebumps cover my body as the cool air hits me in the most sensitive places.

"For weeks, I've been dreaming about how you would look laid out on a bed, ready for me to feast on. I can't wait to taste you," he says in a low voice. His face dips down to my core, tongue dipping out of his mouth as he takes a long, slow lick of my center.

I can't control the moan that erupts from my throat, from my gut. Jake gently teases me with his tongue, focusing on the pulsing nub at my center. He places his finger at my entrance. "God, you're so fucking wet," he says without removing his mouth. The words cause vibrations to pulse through me, sending me so close to the edge. I'm teetering on the brink of sanity and insanity. I'm ready to beg him to just finish me off, to push me completely over the edge.

Jake slides one finger inside me. It's been so long since someone has focused this much attention on me, on my needs. Jake moans against me, again. He whispers, "Fuck, you're so tight."

"Please, Jake."

"Please, what?" he asks, but I can't answer him. I can't form words over the insanely erotic sensations that are flooding my body. Jake demands my attention, my response. "What do you want, Erin?" he asks again.

"You. You inside me. Please," I beg. I know I'm begging for release, but I can't help it.

Jake plunges his finger inside in a fast, possessive rhythm, his tongue doing wonders on my clit. I close my eyes as the stars burst, my body starts to shake, and my core tightens down on his finger. I let out the most unnaturally loud scream as the orgasm rips through my body. I hear myself saying Jake's name over and over again. I couldn't stop it even if I wanted to.

As the tremors start to subside, my breathing is still erratic as

I gulp in large mouthfuls of air. I finally force open my eyes and look up at Jake. The look on his face is primal, fierce. "The fact your neighbors now know my name as the person who just gave you that orgasm makes me want to do it all over again. Right now." I smile in response because my limbs are still Jell-O and my breathing is not anywhere close to normal yet.

"That is so embarrassing," I mumble.

"That, darlin', is so damn hot. It sets the bar pretty damn high for future orgasms. I can't wait to try to top it. Every. Single. Time." Jake pecks a kiss on my lips in between each of those last three words. "Don't move. We are definitely not done yet," he adds as he stands up and starts to remove his clothes.

Jake without clothes is a work of art. Seriously, he should be hanging in a museum somewhere as everyone fawns and drools all over his magnificent body. His chest is broad and perfectly sculpted, and he as a tattoo over his right pectoral. It looks like some sort of military markings, and the dark ink against his tanned skin looks amazing. I can't wait to get a hold of him and explore. None of the guys I've ever dated had a tattoo, and I didn't really care for them before. Before Jake. His tattoo makes me feel like I'm with a real bad boy.

Jake tosses his boxers and stands before me gloriously naked. I look down at his very large, very long shaft jetting out from his groin. I gasp at the sheer size of it.

"What?" he asks.

"I don't think it's gonna fit," I reply all wide-eyed and with a little worry laced in my voice. My only experience with sex was with men who were nowhere near the size of Jake.

He chuckles and starts to climb onto the bed. "Trust me, darlin'. It'll fit. But we'll just take it very, very slow. Okay?"

"Okay," I respond as he takes his place over top of me, gently kissing my lips. My body instantly responds to his touch, his kiss. His kisses hypnotize me in a way that none ever have before.

His hands begin to explore my body again, touching me

everywhere. His touch is calm and gentle, not hurried like it was earlier. I feel safe and cherished in this moment with him.

Jake sits up on his knees and reaches for his wallet. He removes a foil package and sets it on the bed next to me. I look down at his shaft once more as my mouth waters, fingers itching to touch him.

I lean up on my elbows as I reach out and gently touch him. His shaft jumps as my fingers touch the soft, velvety skin. I wrap my hand around it and it appears to get bigger, harder right before my eyes. I look up at Jake and his eyes are closed. The look on his face is one of pure ecstasy so I gently start to pump my hand up and down, slowly and with a little pressure.

Jake moans as his head falls back. That sound coming from his lips encourages me to continue my exploration of his manhood. I want to run my tongue up and down the vein that is pulsing in my hand, but before I can do that, Jake grabs my hand and pulls it off of him. "You keep that up too much longer and we'll never get to the really good part."

Jake's lips seek mine one more time as he lays me back down on the bed. He sheathes himself with the condom and poises himself over the top of me, over my entrance.

"Ready?" he asks. I shake my head, not trusting myself to be able to form words. "We'll go slow, okay? If it hurts too much, I'll stop." Again, I shake my head.

Jake presses the tip of his shaft inside of me. He gently guides himself, very slowly, inch by glorious inch. I gasp as I feel myself stretching to accommodate him.

"Do you want me to stop?" he asks, voice filled with concern.

"No. Don't stop," I tell him. There isn't much pain as I feel myself stretch. It feels magnificent.

When he's all the way in, he kisses my lips. "Okay?"

"Definitely okay. This feels amazing." And that gives him all the encouragement he needs to continue. His pace is slow and gentle. His hands explore my body, and his eyes never leave mine.

Jake changes up our positioning a little so he's kneeling as he drives into me. This position allows him to go even deeper and hit that spot inside of me that makes me moan. The sounds I make seem to drive him further over the edge as he starts to pick up the pace. He spreads my knees further apart as he continues his drive for release. His hand makes its way to my stomach and trails down to my center. He gently rubs the little bundle of nerves between my legs and practically sends me orbiting into another world.

I feel myself tighten around him as my second orgasm of the night takes hold. It's not quite as intense as the first one, but equally as earth-shattering. Jake's name is on my lips as I lose control underneath him. His eyes are locked on mine as he pounds into me a few more times, stills, and loudly moans his own release.

Jake collapses down on top of me, our bodies slick with sweat, as we pant and try to recoup from the exertion together. "That was fucking amazing," he mumbles against my neck.

I couldn't agree with him more. My body is tired and my limbs limp. I couldn't get up and walk out of this room if I tried. I especially can't because Jake is lying on top of me.

Jake rolls over onto his back and just lies there for a moment. A few minutes later, he gets up and goes into the master bathroom to dispose of the condom.

When he comes back in the bedroom, I start to get a little self-conscious. Am I supposed to ask him to stay? Expect him to leave? I have no clue. The only guys I've slept with I was dating. I'm technically not dating Jake. I reach down and grab a hold of the sheet, ready to cover up my body. I feel so exposed lying here for the world to see.

I decide to take a chance and invite him to stay with me. What's the worst that could happen? He will say no or he will stay. When he stands by the bed looking down at me, I flip the sheet open as if in invitation for him to join me. He hesitates but only for a moment. "I have to work tomorrow. I can leave whenever so you can get some sleep; sleep in if you want to."

I yawn as my body begins to relax against his. "What time do you work in the morning?"

"Nine."

"I'll be up way before then. I want you to stay," I say as my eyes lock on his.

Jake leans forward and kisses my lips. "Good. I want to stay," he says as he tucks my much smaller body against his.

Jake's gentle breath on my head, the steady thump of his heart in his chest, and the caress of his fingers on my back are the last things I remember as I drift off into a dreamless sleep.

Chapter 9

Jake

As I start to wake up, I'm instantly aware of two things. One, I am definitely not in my own bed. This one is soft and smells like flowers. And two, there is a very soft hand wrapped around my hard-on. I crack open my eyes and feel like I've been struck by lightning. No, not at the action going on down below, even though that is a pretty damn awesome way to wake up. I'm struck by the sheer beauty of Erin with her hair all wild from sleep. Her makeup-free face is flawless and glowing. Her bare breasts are peeking over the top of the blanket.

"Mornin'," I say as I watch her stroke me.

"Good morning," she says with a shy smile. "There's something that I've wanted to do since last night," she purrs.

Hell yeah! "Well, by all means. Don't let me stop you," I add with a cocky smile. I lace my hands behind my head and just enjoy the show.

Erin runs her tongue down my shaft from the tip to the base. I feel it jump and pulse in her hand. She slowly starts to work her hand up and down, tracing the same path with her tongue and hand. It's a delicious combination as she pleasures me with her mouth.

When she takes me inside of her warm mouth, I almost lift

up off the bed. I've had my fair share of blow jobs before, but the feel of her lush mouth on me almost sends me over the edge and coming instantly.

She moves her mouth up and down—slowly at first and then gradually picking up speed—applying gentle suction from her mouth as she goes. I feel the familiar tightening in my balls and I know I'm close to coming. Erin starts to move faster, sucking harder, and gripping me tighter with her hand. When she reaches down and grabs a hold of my balls, I'm done.

"I'm going to come," I warn her.

Her beautiful green eyes lock on mine and the determination is evident on her face. She tightens her hand further as she pumps and I come with force inside her mouth.

I've seen girls who shy away from the act of blow jobs or of getting anything in their mouth. Erin did neither of those. She welcomed it. If the look in her eyes is any indication, it seems to turn her on even more.

I lace my fingers through her hair as she continues to lick and suck me until I'm going limp in her hand. I lie back with my eyes closed and just enjoy the feeling of her mouth on me. "That was fucking awesome."

"It was my first one," she confesses quietly.

My eyes open and find hers. She has the cutest look on her face. It's a combination of shyness and embarrassment. That look has always been one of my favorites.

"Well, you handled it like a pro. You'd never know it was your first time." I reach down and grab her arms, pulling her up against my chest. "How is it possible that you've never done that before?"

"Well, my past boyfriends never seemed very interested in it. It just never really came up."

"You have been dating the wrong kind of guys then, darlin'," I say with another kiss of her full lips. I can't seem to stop myself from wanting to kiss her.

"You're probably right," she adds.

I look over at the clock and see it's after seven. Just enough time to return the favor, shower, and grab breakfast. Hell, maybe return the favor *in* the shower; you know what they say about two birds and one stone. "Let's take a shower and grab breakfast before I have to go to work."

"Okay," she says as I lead her toward her master bath.

Inside, I turn on the hot water until I see the steam rising up in the air. After adding cold water and adjusting the temperature to a comfortable setting, I turn around and extend my hand to Erin. She doesn't even hesitate to grab a hold of it. I pull her against me, my lips seeking out hers as if entirely on their own.

"I have morning breath," she mumbles as I continue to kiss her.

"I don't care. So do I." She opens her mouth for me and I plunge my tongue inside, devouring her mouth with my own.

I pull her toward the tub and step inside. The water is warm and does wonders against my muscles. I grab a hold of the sides of her head and hold her still as I consume her lush mouth. I quickly remind myself that this moment is for Erin, to return the sexual favor I received this morning when I woke up.

I pull away from her face and guide her back toward the shower wall. She gasps as the cold wall touches her back. "Stay here," I tell her.

I move the showerhead so it's spraying her. I don't want her to get cold, after all. Then I drop to my knees and spread her legs. I use my mouth and fingers to repeat what I did last night. This time, I add a second finger.

Erin's hands are in my hair, gripping my head as she holds on for dear life. That act alone makes me want to bend her over and plunge into her. But, I won't. At least not yet.

I feel her body tense up as I bring her to orgasm. Her moans are sweet music to my ears, and all the encouragement I need as I slow my fingers and tongue to very gentle strokes. Her hands fall from my head and her knees start to buckle. I quickly stand up and

106

grab a hold of her to keep her from sliding down the shower wall.

When I'm sure her legs will hold her up again, I lay gentle kisses along her neck and collarbone and let go of her, turning and grabbing the bar of soap. As I lather up my hands, Erin winds her arms around me, her chest pressed up against my back and rests her head against my mid-back. She sighs heavily, feeling completely relaxed. I love the feel of her body pressed firmly against mine.

As I turn around, I grab her arms and start to lather her up. I use long, firm strokes with my hands to massage the soap into her skin. "Oh my God, that feels so good. I used muscles last night that I didn't even know I had."

I laugh as she rolls her neck from side to side. I start kneading her neck with my fingers, which earns me another delicious moan. I fucking love that sound.

I start to wash up my body as Erin washes her hair. There's something sensual about watching her cleanse herself in the shower. I've taken a few showers with women before, but never actually paid close enough attention to the actual act of showering. It's erotic as hell. Or maybe it's just her.

Once she's finished, I give my hair a quick washing. After all the soap is rinsed, I shut off the water and grab a couple of towels. I wrap the first one around Erin, using my big hands to swiftly dry her body. Once she steps out of the shower, I grab another towel and dry myself off.

Back in her room, I realize I'm going to have to put back on yesterday's clothes. Not that I wore them very long since I put them on after work last night. "Hey, Erin. We'll run by my house so I can change into my uniform and then head uptown for breakfast."

"Is that a question or a demand?" she asks with a slightly raised eyebrow.

I sigh dramatically and decide to rephrase. "So, how about we stop by my house so I can change, and then we'll run uptown for breakfast? How does that sound?"

"That sounds great," she says with an appeasing smile.

It doesn't take me very long to get dressed. Since Erin still has to finish getting dressed and do whatever it is that girls do in the bathroom to get ready for the day, I decide to head downstairs and check my phone. "Hey, I'll head down and wait there, okay?"

"Okay. I'll only be a few more minutes." I don't believe her for a second. What girl ever only takes a few minutes to get ready?

I settle on the couch and flip on the television while I wait. While watching *Sports Center*, Miss Whiskers comes in and rubs against my leg, purring loudly. I'm not really a cat guy. I see myself more as the big dog kind of guy. I try to shoo the cat away, but she's not having it. She jumps up on the couch and makes herself comfy on my lap. Great.

About ten minutes later, Erin comes down, ready to go. Ten minutes. Who knew? "Aww, I see Miss Whiskers has made a new friend," Erin says with a smile as she enters the living room.

"Your cat is bothersome," I tell her, feigning annoyance as I give her a gentle shove off of my lap.

"She is not! Miss Whiskers is a sweetheart," she says, picking the cat up off the couch and placing a kiss on the top of her head before setting her down on the floor. "Besides, she's usually a better judge of character," she smarts off, fighting to keep her smile at bay.

"I guess I'll just have to prove, again, how good of company I can be," I reply before taking her lips with my own. I pull back after only a few seconds, not wanting to get too wrapped up in the kiss, even though there is nothing I'd rather be doing right now. But I know we need to eat before I head to work so I grab both of our coats as we head out toward my truck.

On the drive to my place, Erin is telling me about the upcoming city council meeting she has to attend to give her first month's city library report.

"I'm a little nervous. I'm not a fan of getting up in front of people and talking. Plus, these people ultimately write my paycheck, set my budget for each year, and make decisions on how I spend certain chunks of money and apply for grants."

"You'll be just fine, darlin'. I've been to a few council meetings and they're no big deal. Most of the people there are the council members themselves. Those meetings don't exactly draw a crowd."

"I know, but I'm still nervous."

"Well, don't be," I say as I pull into my driveway. "Wanna come in while I change?"

"Yes. It'll give me a chance to snoop around," she says with a grin.

I help her out of the truck and head toward the back door. "Feel free to snoop around until your little heart is content while I run back to my room and change," I say as I head toward the hall.

While I'm in my room changing, I hear her yell from the living room, "You have a beer sign in your living room."

"Yeah, so? What's your point?"

"You can't have a beer sign in your living room. This isn't a college dorm."

"It's a bachelor pad, darlin'. Same thing."

"You might as well have a keg in the corner of your kitchen and plastic furniture in your living room."

"That would be sweet," I throw back to her down the hall, but honestly, that doesn't hold any appeal to me anymore.

As I'm pulling my service pistol and badge out of the lock box in my nightstand, I hear Erin come in the room behind me. "So this is what your room looks like."

"This is it," I say as I turn toward her, placing my pistol in the holster and clip my badge onto my belt. I walk to her and say, "I'd give you a tour of all the important parts like my bed, but then we wouldn't have time for breakfast before I have to be at the station."

"Too bad. I guess you'll just have to give me a tour another time."

"Deal. Come on, I'm starving. Let's go to the diner." I grab a hold of her small hand and lead her back out to the truck. As much as I'd love to stay and give her a very thorough tour of my bed, I know that would result in calling in sick to work. But damn if I can't think of any better reason to call in sick than to be in bed all day with Erin. Maybe next time.

Maddox and I are cruising toward my parents' house that afternoon to grab some dinner. Sunday is family dinner night and while we work every other weekend, we still try to head out there and grab some of my mom's home-cooked food to-go. Plus, I always love seeing my niece for those few minutes before I have to head back out again. We're heading down the familiar country road when a domestic call comes in. "Three Ten David, you copy?"

"Copy dispatch, go ahead."

"Reports of a domestic dispute at Fourteen Thirty River Bend Road. Caller reportedly has heard arguing all afternoon. Suspect has a history of domestic violence toward his wife. You copy?"

"Yeah, we copy. We're not that far. We're en route now."

"Fourteen Thirty? That's Jim Handy's place, isn't it?" Maddox asks.

"Yeah, I think so. I'm guessing he's drinking again. Connie always had a hard time controlling him when he starts drinking whiskey."

Maddox drives the car toward the Handys' place. They live on the edge of town in a pretty scarcely populated location near the river. If the neighbors heard anything, it must have been pretty loud. The house is run-down and in desperate need of some TLC. There are two old cars parked in the front yard and a broken swing set on the side of the house near the driveway.

"Well, let's go see what the Handys are up to this fine February afternoon," Maddox says as he steps out of the squad car.

I'm right behind him, approaching the front of the car when we hear the words no one wants to hear, especially a cop.

"Stop right there, boys. You come any closer to this house, and I'll shoot you both where you stand."

Shit. "Jim? It's Officer Stevens. You have a gun in that house with you?" I ask, my right hand releasing the snap on my holster.

"Yeah, I gotta gun! This bitch hasn't shut up all damn day about my drinking. I'm sick of her shit. This here gun is the only thing to make her shut up."

I hear Maddox radio in our request for immediate backup and report that a firearm is on the premise. Suspect is now armed, considered very dangerous, and has a hostage.

I stop walking but continue to engage Jim, trying to pinpoint his location on the property.

"We're just here to talk to you, Jim. There's no need to point guns or threaten anyone. Where is Connie?"

"She's right here, crying her eyes out. If she doesn't knock it off real quick, I'm gonna really give her something to cry about."

Maddox slowly approaches my right side and whispers under his breath, "His speech sounds slurred. I'm pretty sure he's in the front room by the door. Notice it's open?"

"Yeah, I agree. How long until backup arrives?"

"ETA ten minutes. Both of the other cars are on location at an accident on the other side of town."

Jim starts to yell at us about getting off his property, his voice becoming more erratic and unhinged.

"We gotta calm him down or this situation is going to escalate quickly."

"I agree. You head around to the back and see if you can gain entrance. I'll make my way up toward the front door."

"Okay. Be careful," Maddox says before he slowly walks toward the side of the house.

"Where's that boy going?"

"He's just making sure there's no one else in the area. Jim, why don't you put that gun down and come out here and talk with me? I know you really don't want to hurt Connie."

"I do. I do want to hurt her. I'm tired of her shit. All's she does is bitch and moan; whine and cry. 'Quit drinking.' 'Stop smoking.' 'You're worthless.' Well, I'm going to show her just how worthless I am."

Well, shit. This situation is escalating quickly and backup is still eight minutes out. If I don't get in there and get that gun out of his hands, who knows what he'll do. "Jim, I'm coming up to the front door. I'm setting my gun down on the hood of the car. See?" Yeah, huge no-no, but it's all I have to work with here. There is a hostage inside with a gun probably pointed to her head. Jim peeks his head out the front window and watches me set my pistol down. "See? It's down. Now, I'm coming up the front walk very slowly. I just want to talk to you. Okay?"

"Don't come inside, boy."

"I won't. I just want to talk to you through the front door. I want to see Connie."

"She's fine! For now!"

I get to the front door and peek inside. The rifle is pointed at Connie's head as I feared. She's crouching on the floor, curled up in a tight ball, and bawling her tired, worn eyes out. "All right, Jim. I need you to put that gun down. You don't want it to accidentally go off and hurt Connie. You'd never hurt your wife like that."

"Shows what you know," he slurs as he takes a drink of whiskey straight out of the bottle.

The good news is that while Jim is talking to me, his hand gets tired and he slowly starts to lower the rifle. It's pointing at a downward angle; still pointed at Connie, but at least not at her head.

"Jim, you're gonna be in a hell of a lot of trouble over this. Why don't you go ahead and put the gun down before someone gets hurt? Don't make it worse than it already is."

I reach down and slowly open the front door. Jim is watching me, but doesn't make a play for pointing his gun at anyone, myself included. When I step inside, I notice movement toward the back of the house. Maddox is inside too, and slowly creeping up on Jim from behind.

I make eye contact with my partner, silently communicating our strategy. He nods to Jim and then points to himself and then points to me, Connie, and the front door. He's telling me that he'll take Jim and try to neutralize the threat, and I am to get Connie out of the house. I give him a very slight head nod, acknowledging the plan, as Jim focuses his attention back on yelling at his wife.

I know I need to get his attention off of her and onto me so Maddox can make his move. "Hey, Jim. Did you see the Super Bowl game a few weeks back?"

My distraction works because Jim looks over at me, relaxes the gun, and gives me a questioning look. "What?"

Just then, Maddox runs into the room, diving at Jim's back. Jim senses the motion behind him and starts to raise his gun. I'm moving and diving toward Connie, just as the gunshot rings out. The only thing I can hear now is the sound of Connie's panicked screams. I land hard on top of her, rolling away with her body in my arms, away from the struggle going on between Maddox and Jim. During the forward motion of my body and trying to protect Connie, I crack my head on the coffee table and instantly see stars. My gut twists and I have to force myself to not vomit. My only thought is getting Connie out of the house.

As I pull her back toward the front door, I notice Maddox easily has the upper hand on Jim. He's straddling Jim's back, pulling both of his arms tightly behind him. The last thing I see before I'm out the front door is Maddox pulling his cuffs from behind his back.

Once I get outside, I keep moving, dragging Connie toward the squad car. She's screaming hysterically, arms waving widely, as she tries to get away from me. "Calm down, Connie. You're safe now."

Connie instantly starts to settle, but I can tell by the wide look in her eyes that she's still scared to death. "Oh my God, you're bleeding!" she exclaims as she reaches up to my head.

The pain in my head is intense, to say the least, but right now I need to focus on making sure Connie wasn't hit by that stray bullet.

As I'm checking her over for any sign of blood or injuries, I see the other two squad cars tear down the road and stop in the street in front of the Handys'. Maddox comes down the front steps with a handcuffed, stumbling Jim. He walks him straight to our squad car and places him in the back seat.

"You all right?" I ask over my shoulder.

"Yeah. You?" Maddox looks at me for the first time since the ordeal started. "Shit, Jake, you're bleeding!"

"I'll be okay. Just bumped my head on the table."

As the emergency service workers come rushing over, I try to stand up. I see stars again and the most intense pain radiates down my entire body. I close my eyes and feel myself starting to fall. Maddox instantly grabs a hold of me and gently helps me down to the ground. "Jake?" he asks, but I can't seem to open my eyes or answer him.

"Shit! Officer down! I need the medic now! Jake's been shot!" I hear Maddox yell, but it seems like he's miles away. The pain in my head is so intense it feels like it might actually explode off of my shoulders. But now there's a new pain too. My arm is tingling and burning and has a wet sensation. Did I get hit by that stray bullet?

That question is the last thought that goes through my mind as I succumb to the darkness around me.

Chapter 10

Erin

I despise painting. If I never have to pick up another paintbrush and roller again, I will be a very happy woman. But when this last coat of paint goes on, my painting projects will officially be over! The last room is my office, den, and library. And once these walls are complete, I can begin constructing those beautiful barn wood shelves I found on Pinterest. Okay, so I can *find* someone to build me those shelves. Maybe Jake can do it? He has proven to be pretty handy around the house, but we haven't exactly gotten to "woodworking" on the list of his many, many talents.

When my phone rings, it's a very welcome reprieve. "Hello?" I answer a little breathless from the exertion of painting these huge walls all day.

"Erin—" I hear someone say, but the line is full of static and noise.

"Hello?" I ask again a couple more times. I'm about ready to hang up. I'm sure the caller will call back when they have a better signal.

"Erin, its Avery. Can you hear me?"

"Hey, Avery. You sound like you're driving through a tunnel. What's up?" I ask, but there's no reply. I start to think that maybe I lost her due to her poor signal. As I start to bring the phone down from my ear, I hear another voice. A male voice.

"Erin, are you there?"

"Yes," I ask starting to get a little concerned at the urgency in his voice.

"Erin, this is Travis. Where are you?"

"Oh, hey, Travis. I'm at home. What's up?" I ask, a little more cheerfully after discovering who it is.

"Erin, Jake's been shot," Travis says, and a cold chill spreads down my spine.

I have no idea how long I stand here, staring at my wall. I struggle to get the thick air in my lungs. It feels like I can't breathe and my vision is blurry. Cold fear takes over my entire body and I start to shake uncontrollably. I slide down onto the floor, my legs no longer able to hold up my too-heavy body. I vaguely hear a voice in the distance yelling my name. I look down and realize I dropped the phone.

When I pick up the phone, I hear myself whisper, "I'm here."

"Nate is almost to your house. You need to get in the car with him, okay, Erin? Can you do that?"

"Yes," I whisper again.

A few moments later, as I listen to Travis as he tries to calm Avery down in the vehicle with him, I hear a heavy pounding on my front door. I can't make myself get up off the floor and go down to answer it.

"Erin?" I hear behind me. Nate is crouching down in front of me a moment later. He takes the phone from my shaking hands and puts it up to his ear. "I've got her. We're on our way," he says into my phone and then clicks it off, dropping it into his coat pocket.

"Where's your coat, Erin?" Nate asks as he helps me stand up. Nate's almost just as big as Jake. He has many of the same striking features—tall, dark, and handsome—but he's not Jake.

Jake. Is Jake still alive? What will I do if he dies?

I focus back on Nate as he half drags, half pulls me down my stairs. He grabs a coat from my closet and helps me put it on. I have enough sense coming back to me to grab my handbag sitting on the foyer table as we walk out the front door. I'm in Nate's car before I know it and we're tearing out of my driveway, heading toward Rivers Edge Health Center. Heading toward Jake.

Inside the hospital, I see the faces, the lights. I hear the voices, the beeping, the pages overhead. But I can't focus on any of that. I only want to see Jake.

Nate drags me into a large waiting corridor where his family is gathered. Elizabeth and Michael are holding hands and sitting on a plastic-covered love seat along the wall. Travis is pacing the length of the room, back and forth and then back again. Avery is curled up against Maddox, who is holding Brooklyn on his lap. Everyone has solemn faces; their fear as evident as the sunshine outside.

When we walk in the room, everyone stands up immediately and rushes to Nate and me. I'm pulled into a very tight embrace with Elizabeth. She starts to softly cry against my head. I want to cry—I probably should cry—but I just can't make the tears come.

"How is he?" Nate asks.

It's Maddox who replies first, "He's stable. Will was just here a few moments ago and said he hadn't come to yet."

"Was Will in the ambulance?" Nate asks.

"Yep. He was awesome through it all. He remained calm and collected the whole time, even after he realized it was his brother lying there."

"So, what happened?" Nate asks Maddox. "When you called, you didn't get out anything more than to say that Jake was shot before all hell broke loose at the house."

"We responded to a domestic call. When we arrived, the man was in the house with a rifle to his wife's head. I went around back to try to gain access to the residence, while Jake stayed up front and talked to the assailant. We both got inside the house about the same time. Jake distracted the assailant while I jumped him from behind, Jake covering the wife. He was able to get her outside immediately and out of harm's way. But, while in the struggle, the gun fired. We both thought it was a wild shot until we got outside." The look on Maddox's face told the story. He was tortured by the incident and the resulting injury to his partner, his best friend.

"When we got outside, I noticed he was bleeding from the back of the head. He was real shaky on his feet and very pale. He started to sweat and looked like he couldn't focus on my face. That's when I looked down and saw the blood all over his arm and uniform sleeve. I realized he was hit by that stray bullet. That's when he blacked out."

The room is silent as everyone absorbs the details of the incident. I feel an arm go around my shoulders, but I have no idea whose it is. I can't stop staring at the floor.

"Honey, are you okay?" I hear and realize the question is directed at me.

I shake my head up and down, but know that until I actually see Jake with my own eyes and know that he's truly okay, I won't be all right. I need to see him, touch him, hold him more than anything right now.

The next thirty minutes feel like days. Horrible days that just drag on and on and on. Cops are in and out of the waiting area, all checking in and seeing if there are any updates on Jake. An older gentleman has been here for about twenty minutes and is sitting in the seat next to Maddox. I overheard conversation that he is their lieutenant.

When a doctor finally comes into the waiting area, the entire Stevens family is up on their feet in a flash.

"I'm Dr. Cambridge. Jake is awake and alert." I feel the breath I'm holding exhale loudly as happiness settles over me. There are audible exhales all around me as everyone takes a moment to breathe again. "The bullet that hit Jake was a flesh wound to the upper left arm. He's going to be fine; sore, but fine. We were able to stitch that up nicely. My biggest concern has been the blow to Jake's head. He was unconscious until just a bit ago and doesn't remember much about the incident after hitting his head. We had to give him a few staples to close up the gash. The CT scan came back clear for bleeding on his brain, but he's nursing a pretty big concussion. We're going to keep him overnight to monitor that, but if all continues to improve, he should be able to go home sometime tomorrow afternoon."

"Thank you so much, Doctor," Michael exclaims as he extends his hand toward the doctor with a smile on his face.

"He's a tough guy. He'll pull through just fine," Dr. Cambridge adds.

"Can we see him?" Elizabeth asks anxiously.

"They're moving him to a room right now. As soon as he's settled, I'll have the nurse come out and get you."

After many "thanks" and handshakes to the doctor, he heads back down the hallway. I wait for the relief to wash over my body, but it doesn't entirely do so. I need to see Jake. I'll be okay when I see Jake.

I sit back down in my chair and Avery comes over and sits next to me. She laces her hand within mine and leans her head against my shoulder. I feel the warmth of friendship wash over me, something I've never really felt before. I've had friends before, but this feels different. This feels deeper.

"He's going to be okay," she whispers.

"Yes. He is," I reply as I close my eyes and rest my head against hers.

"He's too stubborn to really hurt himself too much," she adds with a smile.

I laugh at the truth in her statement. I look down at our linked hands and realize I have tan and chocolate brown paint all over my hands. When I sit up straighter, I realize I'm covered in paint. I'm a hot mess! I'm wearing a pair of big, baggy sweatpants and a sweatshirt that doesn't even match.

"Oh my God, do you have a mirror?" I ask with a panic.

Avery reaches for her bag and pulls out a compact mirror.

When I flip it open, I'm shocked by my unruly appearance. My hair is pulled up in a crazy bun that has pieces of hair sticking out every which way. I'm wearing no makeup and have dark paint splattered all over my face. I am a walking disaster!

I groan at my appearance as I snap the compact shut and hand Avery back the mirror.

"You look fine," she says.

"I look like a disaster!"

"You were in a bit of a hurry when you left the house, Erin. I take it you were painting?"

"Yeah, I was painting my office. I was just starting the second coat when you called. I should head home and clean up."

"No way! You're not leaving."

"I'll let you guys all spend some time with him and then I'll come back up and visit later. You guys need some family time."

"*You* are family too, Erin. Whether you and Jake see it yet or not, you are a part of this family too."

Since I don't really know how to respond, I don't. A few minutes later, a young nurse comes into the waiting room and tells us Jake is ready for visitors. His parents take off down the hallway after the nurse, followed closely behind by his brothers, sister, Maddox, and Brooklyn. I hang back a little bit, not wanting to impose on their family time.

"Get up here," I hear Maddox say. When I look up, he's turned around at the threshold of an open doorway and waiting for me. "He's going to want to see you most of all." Maddox gives me a knowing grin and walks into the room.

As I approach the doorway, I see Jake's parents leaning down and giving him huge hugs and kisses. Brooklyn is trying to get up on the bed, but Maddox grabs her and holds her just out of reach so she can't grab a hold of Jake and hurt him any further. Will, Travis, and Nate all shake his good hand – which fortunately is his right hand - and go to stand over in the corner. Avery practically jumps on the bed, causing Jake to wince in pain at the impact of her body against his. Maddox gently pries her off of her brother and bends down to hug his friend.

When Jake looks up and sees me standing in the doorway, my heart stops beating. Our eyes lock in the most intense moment of my life. I love him. Seeing him lying in that hospital bed, IV hooked up to his arm, bandages wrapped around part of his head and his arm, I realize that I am so over the top in love with Jake Stevens, I can't even think straight. My heart squeezes and crashes against my chest as I take in his slightly battered features.

Jake reaches his good hand out toward me, and that's when the tears finally come. Relief washes over me like a summer rainstorm as I stare into his beautiful crystal-blue eyes. I slowly make my way toward him, no longer aware that there are other people in the hospital room. As I reach out and take his extended hand, he pulls me down onto his bed next to him. He reaches up and gently wipes away the tears on my face.

"Hi," he says with a small smile.

"Hi," I reply, still staring deep into his eyes. "Are you okay?"

Jake pulls me against his big broad chest and wraps his uninjured arm around my shoulders. "I'm perfect now," he says as he inhales my hair deeply.

The Stevens family stays and visits with Jake for another hour until everyone is starting to get hungry. "Come on everyone. Let's head to the Café to grab dinner since the one I was making at home probably isn't edible anymore. Jake, can we bring you back something to eat, dear?"

"No thanks, Mom. I'm going to get some rest. Thanks, though."

One by one, the entire group goes over to Jake and gives him a hug or a handshake. When everyone has filed out of the room, Elizabeth turns to me. "You coming, dear? You're more than welcome. I'm sure you're starving too."

I look between her and Jake. I really want to stay with Jake for a little longer and then head home and clean up. I still feel gross and unpresentable. "Umm, no thank you. I think I'm going to stay here for just a few more minutes and then head home. Thank you so much for the offer."

Mrs. Stevens gives me a knowing smile and waves as she walks out of the hospital room, with the promise to return very soon.

"Come here, you," Jake says as he holds out his good arm for me to sink down into his embrace on the bed. "It's about time they all left," he adds as he places a kiss on the top of my head.

"I can leave too and let you get some rest."

"I don't want you to leave. I want you to stay here with me. I feel better when you're in my arms. Arm," he adds with a cocky smile.

"I can't believe you got shot," I whisper as the tears threaten to spill over my eyes again.

"It was just a graze. I'm fine. My head is fucking killing me though. How bad is the back? Can you see the staples?" I sit up as Jake leans forward. There's a bandage there, but I gently lift it up and peek inside.

"Yeah, that doesn't look so hot. They had to shave a little area around it."

"I figured. It already itches like crazy."

After I snuggle back into Jake's embrace, I take another deep breath and let the feel of his body wash over me. "I'm so glad you are okay. I was so scared when I got that phone call."

"I'm sorry I scared you, darlin'. It's gonna take more than a stray bullet and a coffee table to get rid of me."

I laugh a little before I reply, "Your sister said pretty much the same thing."

He chuckles. "Oh, I bet she did," he says with a big yawn.

"I'm going to head out and let you rest. Besides, I'm in desperate need of a shower."

"I don't want you to leave yet." When I look up at Jake, his eyes are closed. "What were you painting?"

"I was just starting the second coat in my office. I think I have more on my body than I actually got on the walls."

"You look adorable as hell," he mumbles and shifts himself to a more comfortable position, without letting go of me.

As I lie with Jake on the hospital bed, I take in all of the sounds around me. The slow beeping of the machines, the steady drip from the IV pump, the even sounds of Jake's breathing against my head. I'm completely comforted by the feel of his strong arm wrapped around me. It's the only place I want to be - wrapped up in the strong arms of the man I love. That's my last thought as I slowly succumb into a deep sleep.

Chapter 11

Jake

My head is pounding as I slowly wake from a fitful sleep. One arm is aching and has a slight burning feeling. The other arm is pinned. I quickly realize it's pinned under the beautiful redhead that filled my dreams last night.

Yesterday starts to all come back to me at that moment. The dull ache of my arm and head, the gunshot, the hospital room. Thankfully, it's just a flesh wound so I should be able to get out of here today. The doc said the bump on my head is what concerns them the most. But I know I'll be fine if I can get out of here and into my own house. Hell, maybe I can sweet talk a smoking hot redhead to come over and play nursemaid for me. Now, that thought makes me smile.

Erin starts to rouse from sleep, opening her beautiful green eyes and looking up at me.

"Morning, darlin'."

"Good morning." She sits up and looks at my other arm and face, concern etching her beautiful features. "How are you feeling this morning?"

"Better. I'm ready to go home."

"You can go home when the doctor says you're ready to go

home, Jake. You can't overdo this. You'll end up back in here."

"I'm fine. Give me a few Tylenol, and I'm good to go. Come here and give me a kiss."

Erin leans forward and places a gentle kiss on my lips. The kiss goes straight to my groin and I'm hard instantly. "I'm a little sore down here. Maybe you should kiss that too and make it feel a lot better," I say against her lips with a smile.

Erin pulls back, eyes wide, and swats at my good arm. "Behave, you," she says with a laugh.

Just then a knock sounds at the door and Maddox walks in. "Am I interrupting?"

"Yes," I say at the exact same time Erin says, "No."

"I'm going to see about calling a ride so I can run home to shower and change. I'll be back up in a little bit, okay?"

"One of my brothers can take you home, darlin'. Take your time. I'm not going anywhere."

"See that you don't, Mister. Be nice to the nurses." She leans down and gives me another kiss on the lips. As she walks toward the door, she says goodbye to Maddox.

Maddox approaches me and sits down at the seat next to my bed. "How'd you sleep?" he asks.

"Not bad. You?"

"Like shit." Maddox pauses with a pained look on his face. He looks like shit. His hair is sticking up all crazy like he's run his hand through it all night, his eyes are shadowed, and his face hasn't been shaved. It's like he can't decide which side to take on the internal debate going on in his head. "I just can't stop thinking about what we should have done differently."

"Don't. Don't do that. We did everything we were supposed to do. That guy had a gun trained at his wife's head. It was our job to put ourselves in harm's way. To take her place in front of the barrel of that gun. That's the oath we took. We did everything we were supposed to do to keep that woman safe. None of this is your fault, Maddox."

"Deep down I know that, really, I do. But I still can't help but feel guilty over it. I tackled that man and he pulled the trigger."

"That's right, *he* pulled the trigger, not you. So quit this guilt shit. I'd do it all over again, exactly the same way, if I had the choice."

Maddox looks at me a few moments before finally shaking his head. "So, listen. Avery and I were talking about the parties this Saturday night. We're cancelling them in light of your shooting and head injury."

"Hell no, you're not cancelling them! I'm the freaking best man. You can't cancel the party, only I can cancel the party. And I'm not cancelling the party."

"Dude, you were shot and have a concussion."

"I don't care. I'll be fine by Saturday night. Besides, I don't have to drink. I'll be your designated driver."

"You?" Maddox asks, eyebrows arched to the ceiling.

"Yes, me. I'll drive your drunk ass around from stop to stop. I have the whole night planned and everything. I'll be fine."

"Are you sure? Avery will kill me if something happens to you Saturday night."

"Like I said, I'll be fine. My best friend is getting married next weekend. We have a lot to celebrate."

Maddox gives me a grin before he stands up. He walks over to me and bends down for a hug. "I'm so damn glad you are okay, man."

"You can't get rid of me that easily."

"Believe me, I know," he says with a laugh as he heads toward the door. "We'll stop by your place as soon as you get sprung from this joint."

"Deal. Bring the pizza."

"Deal," he says as he walks out of my room.

Maddox's bachelor party is Saturday night. That reminds me, as I grab for my cell phone. I have a stripper to confirm.

A few minutes after I get off the phone confirming Saturday night's entertainment, Nate walks in with a big smile on his face.

"What's up, man?"

"Not much. I was just on my way to the fire station and wanted to drop this off. I thought maybe Erin would be here so I could return it to her," Nate says as he lays her cell phone down on my bedside table.

"How'd you get that?" I ask, and I'll admit, my tone is not very friendly.

"Chill, man. When I went to her house to pick her up and bring her here yesterday, I dropped it in my pocket."

"Oh," I say as I consider his words. "Thanks for picking her up and bringing her. It was nice to see her face."

Nate sits down in the chair Maddox just vacated a bit ago. "I'll be completely honest with you, dude. When I got to her house yesterday, she was a mess. She had this distant, far-off look on her face. I knocked on the front door and when she didn't answer, I just let myself in. I hollered a few times but didn't get a response so I started checking all the rooms. I finally found her upstairs in the office she was painting, clutching her cell phone to her chest. I picked it up and realized Travis was still on the other end. Once I told him we were on our way, I practically had to carry her down the stairs and out the door. She was freaked the hell out. It scared the shit out of me."

I sit here for a few moments, processing what Nate just told me. Was Erin that upset and scared at the thought of something happening to me? Is she going to be able to deal with this side of my life if we were to consider a relationship? I'm a cop one-hundred-and-ten-percent. I can't imagine myself doing anything else, but what if Erin can't handle my occupational hazards because, let's face it, I have them every time I put on my uniform and slip on that badge.

"Well, thanks again for getting her. I just wish I didn't have to upset or worry her. But it's my job, you know?"

"Yeah, I know. If anyone understands that, it's me. I think that's part of the reason I haven't been too worried about settling down and finding a wife. I don't want to leave her a widow. Too many firemen perish in fires every year. It's a scary thought."

"It is," I reply, looking down at the blanket covering my legs.

"So, are you getting serious with Erin?" he asks casually.

I blow out a big breath. "Well, I like her...a lot. We haven't exactly had the 'are we in a relationship' conversation, but the thought of her having one with another guy makes me want to rip someone's face off. And honestly, I'm not interested in seeing anyone else right now either. For the first time, I'm actually considering a relationship with someone. Like a real, call each other all the time, have stupid cutesy nicknames for each other, only have sex with one woman, kind of relationship. What does that say? Am I a pussy?" I ask with an incredulous chuckle.

"A pussy? No. A douchebag? Well, the jury's still out on that one," Nate smarts off with a cocky grin.

"Thanks, little brother," I reply with my own grin.

"No problem. That's what I'm here for." Nate stands and approaches my bed. "To answer your question, I think Erin's a good girl. If you're ready to actually date one girl for a while, I say give it a try. If it doesn't work out, you can always head over to the pub and give all the girls there each a turn in your bed like ol' times."

The thought of that makes my stomach turn. I don't even want to think about spending the night with anyone else but Erin.

"Well, I need to get to the station. Will you make sure Erin gets her phone?"

"Yep."

"Good." Nate leans down and gives me that half hug, half shoulder nudge kind of hug and turns to walk away. "I'm damn glad you're okay, Brother."

"Thanks, Nate. Be careful out there."

"I will," he says as he turns and heads out the door, leaving me to think about all the important things we just talked about. I love my job and understand it could be scary for Erin to adjust to. She's never really had someone in her life that puts her first, well, except her grandma. I just don't want her to run away from me because she can't deal with my job. It's dangerous and daring. Can she handle that?

God, I hope so.

I learned really quick there is nothing on television during the day. I was bored out of my ever-loving mind all day, waiting on the doctors to release me and for Erin to return. She called from her landline after she got home and ended up going into work for a few hours—at my insistence—so I could get some rest. Honestly, I just thought that her being back in her routine and in her element for a little while would do her some good.

Erin arrives just before five to take me home. I've got my bag already packed and am sitting in the chair waiting on the discharge papers when she walks in the door. I'm tired of being cooped up in this little ten-by-ten room and am itching to get the hell out of here.

When she walks in the door, my face lights up like a Christmas tree. She's stunning in her conservative work clothes; all signs of paint have been removed from her morning shower. A shower that I would have loved to have joined her in.

"Hey, you. You look good," she says as she brings her lips down onto mine.

"I always look good, and I'm feeling pretty good. Ready to go home."

Dr. Cambridge comes into the room at that moment, papers in hand. "Well, here you go, Jake. Sign here," he says as he hands me a clipboard with papers. "Now, it's important to take it easy for a week or so. Make sure you keep wearing that sling for the next five days. It'll help. Get plenty of rest and avoid anything that could cause further bumps to your head. If you feel sick again, lightheaded, or dizzy, come back to the Emergency Room right away. Here's your prescription for pain medication. No drinking alcohol or operating heavy machinery while you're on them. Okay?"

"Sounds fine, Doc. I'm ready to go home and relax with my girl."

"He said for you to take it easy," she says with a knowing smile.

"Yeah, but he didn't mean I have to take it *that* easy. That just means you'll have to do all the work, darlin'," I reply with a big, wolfish grin.

"Jake!" she replies, face flaming red with embarrassment.

"Just take it easy and avoid head bumps and you two should be fine," Dr. Cambridge replies with a little chuckle as he walks out of the room.

"Come on, darlin'. I'm ready to go home." I throw my arm over Erin's shoulder as a nurse returns with a wheelchair.

"In," she insists, pointing to the chair.

I want to argue, but I know it's protocol, so I allow the nurse to wheel me out of the hospital, to Erin's vehicle.

An hour later, Erin is fussing over me, again, as I sit on the couch, waiting on Maddox, Avery, and Brooklyn to come over with pizza. "Erin, stop. I'm fine. You don't need to adjust my pillows every two minutes. If I need them adjusted, I'll do it," I say as I make a grab for her hands that are reaching for another pillow.

"I'm sorry. I just want to make sure you're comfortable."

"I'm fine. I promise. You'll be the first one to know if I need something, okay?"

"Okay," she says as she leans down and places another kiss on my lips. Every time she brings me something or adjusts my pillows, I steal a sweet kiss from her lush lips.

"Actually, I do need something."

"What? What do you need?" she replies instantly.

I grab a hold of her hand and bring it down to my groin. "I need some attention right here."

"Jake!" she says as she pulls her hand back. "Be serious!"

"Oh, believe me, darlin'. I am very serious." Erin steps away as a knock sounds on the back door. She takes off out of the room like a rocket, eager to get away from me and my hard-on.

"Uncle Jake!" Brooklyn exclaims as she runs into the living room and stops right in front of me. "Are you better fwom getting shot?"

"I'm working on it, Bean. Come here," I reach out for her with my right arm. "You can sit on my lap on this leg. Just be careful not to hit this arm here, okay?" I say as I point to my left arm.

"Otay. I colored you a pitcher," she says as she holds up the colorful picture of a cat.

"It's a beautiful picture. I'm going to hang it on my fridge."

"Otay. I'll go put it up dere for you," she says as she hops off my lap and runs back into the kitchen.

Avery walks in a few moments later. "How are you feeling, big brother?"

"Good. Erin's fussing over me like Mom so I haven't had a chance to be anything but good," I quip.

"Oh, leave her alone. She was freaked out. We all were."

"Well, I appreciate all of the concern, but I'm fine."

"And for that, I'm happy. I'd be so pissed off at you if you upstaged me at my wedding by dying or something," she sasses with a big smile.

I laugh hard. "Well, we wouldn't want that."

"Maddox says the parties are still on for this Saturday. Is that smart?"

"I'm gonna need this party to get my mind off of the boredom I'm going to be dying from come Saturday. The parties are most definitely on. Besides, it's not every day my little sister gets married to my best friend."

"True," she says with a smile.

Maddox and Erin come into the living room a few moments later, carrying pizza boxes and paper plates. We all pile around the coffee table and dive into the delicious deep-dish pizza. This is so much better than hospital food.

"So, Jake, what exactly do you have planned for Maddox's bachelor party?" Avery asks.

"Nothing too big. Why?"

"Are there going to be strippers?" she asks with a raised eyebrow.

"Why would you think that?" I ask as I take a big bite of pizza.

"Um, because you've been talking about strippers since we got engaged at Christmas."

"What's a stwipper?" Brooklyn asks as she turns her attention from the cartoons on television to the adults sitting around the table. Everyone's face becomes super serious and all eyes roam from face to face, waiting to see who is going to respond to the three-year-old's question.

"It's someone who is going to dance at Daddy's party this weekend. Like the clown at that birthday party you went to a few weeks ago," Avery says.

"Wike a ballerwina?"

"Yep, kinda like a ballerina, Princess," Maddox says. We all laugh as Brooklyn is pacified with the stripper definition and returns her attention back to the television.

"Isn't Holly going to have entertainment at your party?" I ask Avery.

"God, I hope not. I'm not interested in that," she replies.

"Why would she need to see some half-decent-looking guy dance around and strip when she has me and all of my hotness at home? I don't think you girls need to see a stripper. My mom is going to be there and I really don't think she wants to see one." Maddox says, clearly pulling out all the stops.

"Shows you what you know, Maddox. So, I basically understand that it's okay for you to see strippers at your bachelor party, but not okay for Avery to see them at her bachelorette party. Is that correct?" Erin asks with a curious grin on her face.

"Exactly. I'm glad you get it," Maddox replies before taking a big bite of his pizza.

"Oh, I get it all right," Erin says. "And that's very sexist of you. I hope the first thing you think about, as some woman is shaking her naked ta-tas in your face Saturday night, is the image of your future wife with some big, buff, greased-up macho man shaking what God gave him in her face while straddling her lap."

The look on Maddox's face is absolutely fucking priceless. Avery and I die laughing. Avery leans over and high-fives Erin before settling back down to eat her pizza.

"So, we don't need strippers, Jake. I'm good," Maddox mumbles.

After the pizza is devoured, Maddox and Avery hang out for just a short time before taking off to get Bean home, bathed, and in bed for bedtime. Erin has been in the kitchen for the past half hour, cleaning up what little dishes we had and doing some general cleaning.

"Come here, you," I say as I walk into the kitchen.

"You're supposed to be resting. Get back on the couch," she says as she looks up from scrubbing my stove.

"Stop cleaning my kitchen, woman."

"This thing borders on disgusting. I can't believe you cook on this."

"I don't cook on it. It holds my take-out boxes for me." I walk up behind her and snake my good arm around to her belly. I pull her gently back against my body, careful not to wrench my left arm. "It's getting late. Are you staying here with me?"

"I brought a bag, just in case. I fed Miss Whiskers before I went to pick you up at the hospital so she'll be good until the morning."

"Good. Let's head back to my room." I walk over to the back door and throw the lock. Erin waits for me in the doorway and flips the light off for the kitchen as I approach her. I take her hand in my good one and steer her back toward my bedroom.

I realize, as we step inside my room, this is the first time she'll actually spend the night at my place. We stopped by here once, but ended up at her place the night before. "So, how about that tour of my bed that I promised you?" I ask with an ornery grin.

"Better not, Cowboy. You're under doctor's orders to take it easy. You don't exactly have an easy bone in your body."

"Oh, I'm easy, all right."

Erin walks over to me and starts to unbuckle my belt. "That's what I'm talking about."

"No. You're going to sleep tonight, Jake. I'm not going to be responsible for you reinjuring yourself or causing brain damage."

Erin removes my belt, and I'm actually kind of glad she's here to help. I'm not sure how I would undress while using only one arm and unable to throw my shirt up and over my head.

Once my belt is off, Erin helps remove the sling, lifts my shirt to my armpits and gingerly guides my bad arm out of the sleeve of the T-shirt. I lean forward as she gently pulls the shirt over my head, careful not to hit the staples on the back. It's actually quite the production. When the shirt's off, she helps slide my pants down my legs. She looks up at my hard groin and shakes her head.

"Don't blame me for that. You do that to me. I can't help it."

Once she has me down to my boxers, she guides me back toward my bed, pulling the covers down for me. "I'll go get a glass of water and your pain pill. Be right back."

A few minutes later, Erin's back with a full glass of water and my pill. As I take it, I'm treated to the incredible view of Erin undressing. She shucks her pants, socks, sweater, and bra before turning toward my dresser. She opens up a few drawers until she finds my T-shirts. Erin slides one of my old concert shirts over her head, covering up her bare body. My half hard-on becomes a fully-fledged hard-on at the magnificent image of Erin sauntering toward my bed while wearing my too-big-for-her-petite-body shirt. It's seriously an image that wet dreams are made of. And it's now burned into my memory; something I'll be able to think about for the rest of my life.

Erin slides into bed with me, laying her head on the crook of my good arm. She feels absolutely amazing snuggled against me. I don't even care I'm hard and want to ravish her body right now. The feel of her snuggling against me is enough for me for tonight.

"Good night, Jake."

"Night, darlin'," I reply as I run my hand up and down her back and lean forward to kiss the top of her head.

Erin raises her head and kisses my lips. I love the taste of her. It's all sweet and minty. It doesn't take long for the kiss to go from gentle to *holy shit*. I run my tongue along her lips, tasting her. Her hands are wandering up and down my torso. I love the feel of her soft hands on my bare chest.

"As much as I'd love to keep going and finish this the right way, you're probably not going to let me, so we'd better just say good night right now before I can't stop myself anymore."

"I don't feel comfortable having sex tonight, Jake. I'm sorry," she says as she snuggles back tightly against my chest.

"I know. You're probably right. I need to get some rest and you have to work tomorrow."

"Did you just say that I'm right?"

"Don't let that go to your head. Tomorrow I'll be back to being bossy and domineering. Tonight, I just want to hold you as I fall asleep."

"I can handle that. Good night, Jake."

"Night, darlin'," I mumble as I carefully rest my head against the top of hers. I inhale her intoxicating tropical shampoo and stroke my hand against her back. I feel her gentle breath against my neck. In the past, I've never been a big snuggler. Once I spent the night with a woman, I was out of there as quick as I could. Sometimes I went back for seconds, sometimes not. But with Erin lying next to me, against me, I feel content. Calm. Happy. That's the last thought I recall as I drift off to sleep with my girl in my arms.

For the next three nights, Erin and I settle into a comfortable routine. She runs to her place after work, grabs a fresh change of clothes, feeds her cat, and then comes over to my place. When she gets here, we make dinner, eat in the living room, and hang out. She generally reads while I watch some sporting event or an action movie on television. When its bedtime, we fall asleep in each other's arms until morning, where we do it all over again.

To say I'm bored come Friday is an understatement. My days are filled with watching television or entertaining company. Maddox comes over with Bean on his days off and bitches about the rookie he's partnered up with until my return.

"Seriously, I can't even say 'shit' without him either throwing my 'foul mouth' back in my face or quoting scriptures. It drives me crazy. It drives me fucking crazy!"

"Maybe you'll start appreciating me a little more now, man. You didn't realize how good you had it until I'm not there every day to keep track of you."

"This straight and narrow shit is for the birds." We both laugh. "So, what's the plan for the party tomorrow night?"

"Just be ready at six. We're gonna stop by and pick you up on our way to Laverne's. Dinner is our first stop. We'll end up at Jack's at the end of the night. And don't worry about driving or anything. I'll be picking you up and chauffeuring you around since I can't drink yet."

"Are you still planning the whole stripper thing? 'Cause I'll be honest, I'm not exactly excited about Avery having a stripper. Maybe we should skip it and then she'll do the same."

"Don't be a pussy. And trust me. You'll have a great time with what I have planned," I say with a big smile.

Maddox stands up and grabs his coat. "Trust you. Last time I did that, I wound up naked, wearing a sombrero and cowboy boots, and dancing on that table for tips."

I laugh hard at the memory of our first weekend home, following boot camp, that involved a handful of girls and a whole lot of tequila. "Who knew you had such moves, my friend."

Maddox laughs. "Let's just keep my clothes on this time. I doubt your sister would appreciate that, and I'd prefer to actually live to see my wedding day."

"Deal."

"Big plans tonight?" Maddox asks as he heads toward the door.

"I'm going crazy in this house. I'm planning on taking Erin out to dinner and then maybe a movie. Anything to not stare at these walls for another night."

"Well, have fun, man. If you need anything, let me know."

"Will do. See you tomorrow at six," I say as Maddox heads out the door with a wave.

Well, I have about three hours until Erin gets here, so plenty of time to plan a date night. Now, I just have to decide what to do. Dinner is a must but I'm starting to rethink the movie idea. The last thing I want to do is sit and watch more mindless TV or another movie. So, now what?

"Honey, I'm home," Erin says as she comes in the back door and sets down her bag on the kitchen table.

I'm in the kitchen to greet her a few moments later. "Hi," I say as I lean forward and give her a kiss.

"Hi, yourself," she murmurs against my lips. "Hey, where is

your sling?"

"I was sick of it. It's been five days and I was tired of it restricting my movements. It had to go," I say as I move my shoulder around like I'm a pitcher warming up.

"It doesn't hurt?"

"Nope. It actually feels better having that thing off."

Erin goes over and grabs a glass out of the cabinet and fills it with tap water. "So, what are we doing tonight?" she asks as she takes a drink of water.

"Well, I thought we'd go somewhere for dinner and then maybe bowling," I say as I reach out for her hand.

"Bowling? No way! You're supposed to be taking it easy."

"Bowling isn't strenuous. I only need one hand to throw a ball down the lane and my right arm is fine. Besides, my strength is coming back in my left arm and it doesn't hurt as much to move it around. I'm on the mend, babe."

"But you have a head injury."

"And I'm not bouncing the bowling balls off my head, darlin'. I'll be fine. I want to do something fun with you." I stand right in front of her, link my fingers into hers and lean down to bring my lips to hers. "I promise I'll take it easy."

She sighs against my lips. "If I see one sign of you being in pain, we're leaving, Jacob Andrew Stevens," she says in her best stern librarian voice.

"I love it when you get all bossy. And you have a deal. If I misbehave, you can bring me home and punish me."

She laughs against my lips and it sends zings of lust straight down south to my belt. I'd much rather throw her over my shoulder and carry her to my bed, but I know there's no way she'll go for that quite yet. Soon. Very soon. "Let's go get ready for dinner then."

Erin throws me an "Okay" over her shoulder as she heads back toward my room. Oh, how I wish she was heading back there to stay. I never, ever thought I'd be okay with that thought. But the image of Erin walking back to my room with a bag makes me happier than I've ever been. Now I just need to figure out how to make it a permanent image.

We opt to go to Slices Pizzeria for supper, since our last outing to Laverne's Steakhouse didn't go so well with Lauren working there. If I'm being honest with myself, I could have troubles in just about every restaurant in this city and several around it. I've had my share of short-term girlfriends and one-night stands, but for the first time in my life, I'm actually considering changing that entire image. I might be actually considering my first major relationship with Erin. Okay, so I *have* been considering it for a few days now.

Technically, I'm probably already in one with her. I'm not seeing anyone else, and as far as I know, neither is she. Which, now, makes me think about Erin dating someone else. Does she think we're in a relationship? That we're monogamous?

"Hey, so I wanted to ask... I mean, I wanted to let you know that I'm not seeing anyone. You know that, right?"

Erin looks over with a curious look on her face. The wheels inside that beautiful head are definitely turning now. "Yeah, I guess I assumed you weren't seeing anyone else. Why? Are you seeing someone else?" The panicked look on her face betrays the cool and calm exterior she generally tries to keep in place.

"Hell no! I just wanted to make sure you knew that I'm with you and you alone. That's all."

"Oh, okay. That's good."

"And you? Are you seeing anyone else?"

Erin laughs. "Uhhh, no. There's no one else, Jake. I wasn't even looking for a relationship when you came along."

"Why? Why weren't you looking for a relationship?"

"Well, they just never seemed to work out so well for me in the past. The guys I've always dated were more interested in establishing their careers or their schooling to make me much of a priority. I always said when it was time for my next relationship, I would make sure I was a priority in his life."

"Do you feel like a priority in mine?"

She doesn't answer me right away, which makes me a little nervous and uneasy. "Erin, answer me."

"I do. I just... I just don't know how long it will last," she says so quietly that I almost can't hear her.

I pull into the pizzeria, throw my truck in park, and turn to look at her. "Erin. I'll be the first to admit that I haven't exactly had many relationships in my life. I've never done long term or serious. You are the first girl who has made me feel like I want to change that, and I want to be a better person for you. I want to try a real relationship with you and only you."

I search her eyes, looking for any sign that she understands what I'm telling her. She finally smiles a little smile and gives me a small "Okay."

"Just promise me you will always tell me what you're feeling and answer me honestly. Even if you think it's something I don't want to hear, please just always say it. Deal?"

"Deal."

"All right," I say as I lean over and kiss her soft lips. "Let's go get some pizza. I'm starving."

Inside, we're seated at a booth in the busy pizzeria. The lighting is bright and the décor is trendy. There are old road signs and local memorabilia hanging from every available wall space in the large open room. Our server looks a little frazzled as she hustles from booth to booth taking drink and pizza orders. When she finally makes it over to our booth, she takes one look at me and her whole demeanor changes. She instantly smiles and starts to bat her eyelashes. I used to love this reaction from ladies wherever I went. Now, it's annoying as hell, and I don't want Erin to bear witness to it.

"Hey, Jake. How have you been?"

"Uh, good. You?" I don't really care, but I don't want to be an ass. Plus, I recognize her a little but can't place from where. That never works out so well in the long run.

"Oh, you know. Same ol', same ol'. I haven't seen you at Jack's lately." She turns her flirty face into one of concern. "I heard you got shot! Oh my gosh, I'm soooo glad you're okay!" She runs her hand up my forearm to my bicep, stopping on top of the bandage. "Does it hurt?"

"Not too much anymore," I say as I start to pull back, feeling all sorts of uncomfortable in the current situation—with her hand on me.

Pizza Girl has yet to even acknowledge Erin sitting right next to me. When I look over at Erin, she has a look on her face that clearly shows her disgust and shock at the server's boldness. I reach over and link my fingers with hers.

"So, I'm off tomorrow night. I hear its Maddox's bachelor party. Maybe you can give me a call after the party starts to wind down. I'd be happy to continue to entertain you," she says and bats her eyelashes again at me.

I hear Erin's audible gasp as she tries to pull back her hand. Oh, hell no! "Yeah, sorry—" I look down at her name tag and see the name Jen. "Sorry, Jen. But I'll only be going home tomorrow night, or any other night, with my girlfriend here. This is Erin."

Jen seems to notice Erin sitting next to me for the first time and gives her a quick once-over. I feel Erin pulling away from me and I tug her hand over to my leg, steeling my grip on her hand so she can't pull away.

"Girlfriend?" she asks. "Well, I'm sure that'll last a few more days. When you're tired of the good girl librarian, give me a call, Jake. We always had a great time together." With that, Jen turns and walks away from our table.

Holy Shitballs! Could this possibly get any worse? I turn quickly to Erin, but she's looking down and not making eye contact with me. I have no clue what to say.

"Erin—" I start but she interrupts.

"I'm not feeling so well, Jake. Can we just head out?"

"Of course. I'm not hungry anymore for pizza. Let's go get something somewhere else."

I grab Erin's coat as we slide out of the booth. I try not to even look at Jen, but she's standing near the servers' station by the entrance to the dining room. She's clearly talking about me or Erin with another server. I reach down and grab a hold of Erin's hand and lace my fingers through hers. She doesn't pull away, but I can tell something's different. She doesn't respond the way she normally does when we hold hands.

Outside in the cool air, I feel like I can't breathe. She's obviously pissed, and rightfully so. I just don't know how to fix this and make it right.

Once we're settled in the truck, I turn to her and try to talk. "Okay, so obviously I know that girl too. I'm sorry about what she said."

"You can't help the way some people react to me or us. You've slept with half this town, Jake. I just don't know how to deal with that. Or, honestly, even if I can," she whispers.

Panic starts to set in at the thought of losing Erin over my wayward past. "First off, I haven't slept with half the town, Erin." Her eyes crash into mine, eyebrow shooting straight to the roof of the truck. "And second, what the hell does that mean? You don't know if you can deal with what?"

She sighs again and turns away. "I like quiet. Simple. I don't know if I can handle everyone being all up in my business, Jake. I don't want them talking about me, knowing things about my personal life. I want privacy, Jake."

"I can't help it if someone talks about you or me any more than you can help it. I can't change my past, Erin. I can only help my future. And right now, all I want is to see what the future holds for you and me."

She stares at me for a few minutes, mulling over my words in her beautiful head. I find myself holding my breath, waiting for her to respond.

"Do I sound like a crazy possessive girlfriend, right now?" she asks with a small smile.

I smile back at her. "You sound like someone who doesn't

want everyone knowing our business. And that's just what this is to me, our business. What happens between you and me is ours, not hers or anyone else's. You are beautiful, smart, funny, stubborn as hell, and ungodly sexy. I don't care if no one else can see that. That's actually good for me because then I have you all to myself and don't have constant competition to fight off."

She laughs. "You don't have to worry about that. I haven't had anyone beating down my door for...well, ever."

I lean forward and brush my lips across hers because, frankly, I can't help but want to feel her lips on mine. "Let's eat," I finally say after a very satisfying kiss that leaves me yearning for more.

"Is that a question or a demand?" she asks, irritation laced in her question.

"Both. I'm starving. I know you're starving, so let's go eat." I throw my truck in reverse and head out of the pizzeria parking lot.

I couldn't care less where we go to eat, just as long as we're there together. In the past, I've never really enjoyed sharing meals with women. The forced small talk and the cheesy time-filling, question-and-answer session; it's all a big waste of time. At least, that's how I felt during it, so I avoided it at all costs. But not with Erin. With Erin, I want to spend as much time with her as possible, getting to know what makes her happy and sad. I just want to spend it with Erin.

Chapter 12

Erin

Despite being snuggled up against Jake all night, I didn't get the best night of sleep. My mind kept repeating what that server said to Jake about me being a good girl librarian. That's my job. So maybe I can't be a bad girl librarian out in public. *But* I can be a bad girl librarian at home. Right?

So, after Jake and I eat a quick bite of Cinnamon Toast Crunch for breakfast and down a pot of coffee, I decide that it's time for me, Erin Sophia Anderson, to channel my inner bad girl.

I don't have any close friends here really, and the thought of doing this alone terrifies me on more than one level. So as soon as I can come up with an excuse to get out of the house without Jake— telling him I got called in to help my part-timer with a few things at the library—I take off toward Avery and Maddox's. I need girl help, and I need it now!

When I pull into their driveway, I feel the nerves take root deep in my belly. I've always been more of the Plain Jane type and that's always worked for me. Case in point: my white cotton bras and white cotton panties. Living dangerously has always been wearing a pair of printed cotton panties. Stand back, folks...Erin Anderson is wearing pastel plaids! But now I want to be sexy and desired for myself as much as for Jake.

Jake has never, ever made me feel less than desirable. If anything, he makes me feel completely and utterly desirable and appreciated, despite my basic, Plain Jane appearance. But this is something I want to do for me. I need to do this for me.

So, I pull up my big girl panties, raise my chin, and walk up Avery and Maddox's front walk toward their door. It doesn't take Maddox but a few seconds to answer as soon as I knock. "Hi, Maddox. Is Avery here?"

"Yeah, come on in," he says as he opens the door widely for me to enter.

"Ave, Erin's here," he yells as he shuts the door behind me.

A few moments later, Avery comes down the stairs with a big smile on her face. "Well, this is a pleasant surprise. I wasn't expecting to see you until the party tonight."

"That's actually why I'm here. I need your help with something." I look at Maddox, not really wanting to continue this conversation while he's standing here.

"I see where I'm not wanted. I'll go up and check on Brooklyn," Maddox says as he heads up the stairs, taking them two at a time.

"So, what's up? You're still coming tonight, right?' she asks with a little panic laced in her voice.

"Yes, I'm still coming. I just need to ask you a question."

"Okay, shoot."

"Ummm, okay, so if you wanted to seduce Maddox, what exactly would you wear?" I ask, my voice very small. I can't even make eye contact with her for fear that I'll die of embarrassment.

"Well, every guy has different tastes and likes. I'm assuming you're talking about lingerie, right?" Avery waits while I shake my head up and down.

"Okay, well Maddox likes black lace so I tend to wear black lace matching bra and panty sets. I also have this black corset thingy that makes him lose his mind every time I wear it. It comes in very handy when I need to get him to agree easily to something," she adds with a gleam in her eyes.

"Okay. That helps. Thanks for the suggestions, Avery. I'll see you tonight," I say as I turn toward the door.

"Wait. Where are you going?" she asks as she turns me back around to face her. "First off, let's pretend that you're not asking me this with the sole purpose of seducing my brother. Let's go with the name Jeff. And *Jeff* is not my brother, okay?" she asks with a laugh. "Maddox?" she yells up the stairs.

Maddox appears a few moments later and descends the stairs. "What's up, babe?"

"I'm making a trip to the mall with Erin. Can you watch Brooklyn for a bit while I run out?"

"You're going now? The bachelor and bachelorette parties are in a few hours," he comments as he checks the time on his watch.

"I know. I'll be back in plenty of time. We're running to the lingerie store at the mall in St. Charles," Avery says as she grabs her coat.

"Really?" he asks, eyebrows raised with a wolfish grin spread wide across his handsome face. "Do you want my credit card?"

"I already have your checkbook, love." Avery leans in and kisses Maddox passionately before turning toward me. "We'll be back shortly. Love you, babe."

"Take your time. Browse around and make sure you check everything out thoroughly. If you can't decide between a few things, just get them all. You can model them later," he says with a big smile. "Love you too," he mumbles as he leans in and gives Avery another very passionate kiss that promises dirty things later tonight. With that we're out the door and heading toward the mall in St. Charles to purchase something sexy for my man...*Jeff.*

The thirty-minute ride to St. Charles goes quickly when you're listening to Avery talk about next week's big wedding. In the past, I hated getting into wedding conversations with bride-to-bes. I never cared about their choice of flowers or dresses, the venues or the menu. But when Avery is filling me in on every detail of her big day, I can't help but feel the excitement right along with her. I'm truly excited and happy for her and Maddox.

"Which reminds me, I have a question for you. Will you help be my personal assistant next Saturday? I realize now that I can't do everything myself, and I need to relinquish some control over certain aspects of the wedding."

"What kind of things?" I ask.

"Well, help me make sure the guys are ready and where they're supposed to be. Pin a few boutonnieres and corsages. Make sure everything is set up and ready to go before the guests arrive at the church."

"I'd be honored to do that for you. Anything I can do to help you!"

"Really? Okay, thank you soooo much! I know it's a small wedding, but I'm terrified something major is going to go wrong or I'm forgetting a major detail. If I have someone I know and trust looking over some of those details, I know I'll be able to settle down and relax a little that day."

Avery trusts me? That thought brings a smile to my face. We haven't known each other very long, but in the short amount of time I've known her, I've come to think of her as a good friend. A sister. Heck, maybe someday we will be sisters.

WHOOOOA! Let's not get ahead of ourselves, Erin. Jake and I aren't even close to wedding bells so let's hold the horse and back it up a bit.

When we pull into the packed mall parking lot, Avery is fortunate enough that someone is backing out of an up-front space near the entrance closest to the lingerie store. She's practically pulling me along behind her as we make our way inside.

It doesn't take but a few minutes before we're walking through the open doors of the store. Everywhere I look are bras and panties; negligees and teddies. There are so many styles to choose from that my brain is on total overload as I scan the variety of undergarments.

"Come over here," Avery says as she drags me to a section filled with bra and panty sets.

"What size are you?" she asks.

"Small underwear and a 32C cup," I say as I try to hide my face behind my hair, conveniently hanging down in my face.

"You seem like a very simple, but elegant woman. I think you should go timeless and classic."

"Okay."

"Sure, you can go all super-slut and throw on some lace garters and crotchless panties—and I'm sure 'Jeff' would appreciate that—but I think you would feel more comfortable in something less scandalous."

"I agree. So what does that leave us with?"

"This!" Avery exclaims as she holds up a black-and-white satin and lace bra. The basic bra is white satin that feels like silk to the touch. There are touches of thin black lace over the cup of the bra and it even has a little red heart hanging from the center between the cups. I'll admit, it's beautiful.

"I like it."

"I think it's very *you*. It's classic and sexy but with an edge. And here," Avery says as she digs in the drawer full of matching panties. "There are several different styles of panties, but I think *these* are hot!" Avery holds up a pair of white satin and black lace boy-cut underwear. "You won't have to worry about wedgies all night long with this cut. Boy cut is super cute and will flatter your firm butt."

"I have a firm butt?" I ask with a raised eyebrow.

"Of course you have a firm butt! That's like the first thing I noticed when Jake brought you over the night we moved."

Well then.

"Go try these on!" she exclaims as she drags me toward the dressing rooms in back.

When I get inside the dressing room—and thank you, Jesus,

that Avery didn't insist on coming in with me—I stand and stare at the undergarments in my hands. I can do this. I can be sexy for my man!

The soft satin feels amazing against my skin. I've always worn whatever cheap Target bras I could find, but I have to admit this material is amazing. The black lace is a stark contrast to my skin tone and the white satin is thin enough that you can see the pink outline of my nipples. As I slide on the matching panties, I can't help but already feel the difference that a pair of great underwear makes. I feel instantly sexy. Desirable. A vixen.

As I look at the back, I have to agree with Avery. My butt looks pretty damn good in these!

"How do they look?" Avery asks through the closed door of the dressing room.

"Amazing. I can't believe I haven't made purchases like this before. I'm definitely getting them!"

"And 'Jeff' will die of heart failure when he strips you out of your clothes later tonight," she says through the door with a chuckle. "Since you're all set, I'm going to go find my man a little something to discover later on tonight. I'll meet you up front at the register."

As I dress back in my basic bra and panties, I can't help the huge smile that is spread across my face. I can't wait for Jake to make his own discovery later tonight too.

The limo pulls up in front of my house at six o'clock. Before I can even get my door locked, a half-dozen girls are pouring out of the sunroof and doors of the limo. We're a small group tonight which includes Avery, her best friend, Holly, who planned the party, Maddox's sister, Jessica, his mom, Avery's mom, and three girls who went to high school with Avery and Holly. They immediately introduced themselves as Amber, Cara, and Robin, and of course, me.

I stumble a little in the heels I'm wearing for the evening. I am *so* not used to wearing heels. I'm more of a flats girl for work, but Avery convinced me these sexy black pumps were the way to go. So, after sliding into a pair of dark skinny jeans and a black sweater with a very deep plunge in the front *and* back that is so tight it's almost hard to breathe, I put on the borrowed black pumps and made my way—very carefully—down the front steps of my house.

My hair id down in soft curls that extend past my shoulders and my makeup is soft yet sultry. I'll admit...I look good.

After piling in the limo, which Holly rented so no one had to drive from stop to stop while drinking, I was handed a glass of bubbly champagne. It's been a pretty long time since I've had champagne, so I start to feel the effects of the mixture of bubbles and alcohol after my first glass.

Our first stop is to St. Charles for dinner. We're heading to this seafood place that Maddox and Avery went to on their first date—when they were still sneaking around and hiding from everyone. It's a nice little place with mismatched everything. Avery right away tells everyone the story about the hostess, who was working that night several months ago, and was flat-out hitting on Maddox in front of her. I laugh along with her dramatic and energetic version of the story, but it makes me think of my pizza date last night with Jake. It actually feels good to know that I'm not the only one who gets ignored while the man gets propositioned.

I've been told that after dinner we will hit a few bars, have a few drinks, dance, and end up at Jack's Pub at the end of the night. I'm not sure exactly what the guys are up to tonight. Jake was pretty vague about it, and I didn't want to push the subject too far. He did mention, though, he would be seeing me by the end of the night.

I'm having a great time at dinner. It feels like I've been friends with these women forever. We all laugh and joke and carry on like friends do. Even Mrs. Stevens and Mrs. Jackson join in the fun by sharing jokes and stories that have us practically rolling on the ground laughing, with tears streaming down our faces.

Our first stop after dinner is to a country bar in St. Charles. I've never been a big fan of country music and have no clue how to line dance, but the girls seem excited so I just go with it.

After the first rounds of drinks are purchased, Holly announced that the "games" are beginning.

"So, here's the deal. Avery has a few games to play tonight. First, we're going to have a Bachelorette Scavenger Hunt! Here's the list of all the 'goodies' Avery needs to collect or tasks she must complete by midnight tonight. We have one more stop here in St. Charles before we head back to Rivers Edge. Once we're at Rivers Edge, we'll hit up the saloon first and end the night at Jack's, where we have some very special end-of-the-night partying to do," Holly says with a wink.

"Okay, so first on the list is find a guy to buy you a shot at each stop," Mrs. Stevens says. "That'll be easy. Excuse me, young man," Mrs. Stevens says as she turns to the first guy walking past our group. "It's my daughter's bachelorette party. Would you like to buy her a shot?"

"Mother!" Avery exclaims, looking horrified.

"What? He's cute. Let the boy buy you a shot!"

I drop my little penis straw into my draft beer and take a big swig. Oh, this is going to be a great night! I look over the rest of the scavenger hunt list. Avery has to find a guy to serenade her with a song, write her name in lipstick on some guy's chest, get a guy's phone number on a bar napkin, be the only girl on the dance floor full of guys, body shot off of a guy's stomach, and talk the bartender into giving her an interesting souvenir at each stop along the way. I can't forget that she has to distribute condoms to three different guys at each of our four stops. Oh, and did I mention she has to offer a condom demonstration with each one?

All I can say is thank goodness it's her and not me!

Chapter 13

Jake

At six sharp, I'm pulling into the driveway of my best friend and sister's house to pick up Maddox. I have Nate, James, and Maddox's brother, Aiden, squeezed in the back seat of Maddox's crew cab like sardines. My dad has Maddox's dad, Will, Travis, and our cousin, Barry, following behind us in my mom's car. The other guys from the force or friends of Maddox's are meeting us at Jack's Pub after dinner.

I wanted dinner to be small with just a few family members and close friends. I'm also footing that bill, so smaller works better with the budget. We are fortunate enough to get the back part of the dining room at Laverne's Steakhouse reserved for tonight. Usually, since Laverne's is the best Saturday night dinner location in Rivers Edge, they use the back part for regular seating to accommodate the crowd. But since I went to school with Pete, I was able to pull a few strings.

When we walk inside, of course, Lauren is the hostess. She looks up at the big group of guys and flashes her best "do me" smile as she looks from guy to guy. I can see her checking everyone out like dessert at some man buffet. When I walk up to the booth, her smile falters as she looks up at me but doesn't disappear completely from her face.

"We have a reservation for the back room."

"Oh, yes. The bachelor party." Lauren purrs as she grabs a stack of menus, and announces, "Right this way, gentlemen." As she saunters to the back, her hips sway so far to the left and right that I'm surprised she doesn't throw a hip out of whack. She shows us to our table and starts to place a menu at each setting, leaning over seductively and giving the room as many full cleavage shots as she can get in.

"There you are, gentlemen. Will there be anything else?" she asks and bats her eyelashes.

"Nope, we're good," I reply and turn away from her. Lauren huffs off and we all take our seats around the large table.

Two waiters arrive at our table a few moments later. I order two pitchers of beer and a bunch of appetizers to get us started. As soon as the waiters return with our first round of drinks, I take the opportunity to say a few words. "Gentlemen, tonight is about celebrating Maddox's last weekend as a bachelor. Next Saturday, he will be marrying my little sister. I couldn't picture Avery marrying a better man than Maddox. So, let's raise our beers and toast our friend, son, and brother, Maddox Jackson. And may he remember how much we love him when he's puking his guts up tomorrow morning."

I hear a resounding "Hear! Hear!" and "To Maddox!" from around the table, mixed with laughter. Everyone takes a drink of their beer and the conversation starts to flow. As much as I want to drink a beer with my family and friends, I stick with Coke for the night. I'm also itching to buy Maddox his first shot of the night, but I definitely want to make sure the guys all get plenty of food in them before they hit the hard stuff.

After everyone orders their dinner, the conversation quickly turns to women. Everyone is teasing Maddox about jumping ship, following the straight and narrow, or crossing over to the dark side. Maddox sits there and smiles the entire time as the fellas razz him about giving up his bachelorhood.

"You guys will understand someday," he says with a small smile that lights up his face.

"That's right. There's nothing better than the love of a good woman," my dad chimes in as he raises his glass toward Maddox like a salute. "And you have a damn good one, if I do say so myself," he adds with a wink.

"I agree, Son. Just remember that marriage is all about give and take. You will give and she will take," Maddox's dad says with a laugh.

"That is a very true statement," my dad throws in.

"I can't wait for the first time I hear 'Yes, dear' come out of your mouth," I add.

"Or what about 'You're right.' I bet that one will burn his tongue," Nate chimes in.

"And we all know Avery well enough to know that dear ol' Maddox here will be saying that *a lot*!" Travis quips.

"I will gladly say it if the results get her naked at the end of the night, my friends."

Instantly, the table erupts into groans and sighs. Maddox laughs as half the table reminds him that she's their sister.

"I should punch you for that," I mumble as I take another drink of my Coke, wishing it had a little Jack in it at that moment. I know Avery has sex, obviously—she has my niece—but I still don't want to picture it or think about it or hear it. There are just some lines that brothers and sisters should never, ever cross.

After our steaks are consumed and the bill is paid, the guys and I all file out of the restaurant and head toward our vehicles. All of the guys threw in some money to cover a generous tip, and both dads tried to slip me some money on the sly, but I didn't want it. I wanted to do this for Maddox tonight. Before I can get out the front door with the rest of the guys, Lauren stops me.

"So do you have entertainment lined up for this party?"

"Why?" I ask, curious as to where she's going with this.

"Well, I'd be more than happy to come by after work and help entertain you and your friends," she purrs as if everything that's happened between us—which nothing happened between us, much to her displeasure—is all forgotten.

I take in her plain white button-up shirt and tight black skirt. She's not bad-looking, really. Actually, she's pretty hot, but I just don't want her anywhere near the pub tonight. "Thanks for the offer, but we're all set for tonight," I say as I turn and push open the door. "Have a good night."

"Are you still seeing that girl you brought here?"

I stop and turn back around to face her. "Not that it's any of your business, but yes."

"Well, when you get tired of her, give me a call."

"Who says I'm going to get tired of her?" I throw back, instantly insulted on Erin's behalf.

"Oh, everyone. No one believes for a second that you'll be in this relationship with her longer than a few weeks. You'll get bored, Jake, and move on, just like you always do," she says as she turns back around and walks away.

I stand there for a minute before I hear Nate over my shoulder. "You coming, man?"

"Yep." I turn and head toward the truck, my mind processing what Lauren just said. True, I may not have been a relationship kinda guy in the past, but Erin makes me want to explore that side and be that guy. I want to be with her tonight, tomorrow, and maybe even forever. And that thought doesn't scare me as much as it used to. It actually feels pretty damn good.

After we hit every bar in Rivers Edge, we reach our final destination around eleven. Maddox and the rest of the guys are well on their way to being completely hammered. I've been shoving shot after shot into his hand all night long. As long as I'm driving him, I don't care how much he drinks tonight because I know he'll get home in one piece.

There are two rooms in the back of Jack's Pub that not too

many people know about. We are occupying the larger of the two rooms for the evening that houses an extra pool table in it, and Avery is now occupying the smaller one with just a few extra tables and chairs inside. As far as I know, neither Maddox nor Avery knows the other one is here somewhere. It's all part of the master plan that Holly and I came up with.

Gabe brought in one of his extra bartenders to solely serve our party for the night. The drinks and shots are flowing freely, everyone is laughing and having a great time, and it's almost time for the entertainment to arrive. Several of our fellow officers are here—well, those who didn't get stuck working tonight—as well as a few of our superiors. A handful of local guys we've become friends with or went to school with are also here for the big party.

Everyone seems to be having a great time, buying drinks and shots for Maddox, and asking me when the strippers will be there. It's getting pretty late into the evening and everyone is starting to get a little rowdy. My brothers are shooting pool, which is where I'd love to be, but I'm keeping a close eye on Maddox for the night. I'm trying to avoid distractions like a pool game. The dads are even still hanging with us, sitting in the back nursing a few beers and chatting about cars and work.

When Gabe comes into the private room at eleven thirty, he has a sour look on his face. "Hey, man. Can I talk to you real quick?"

"Sure. What's up?" I ask as we head over to the corner of the room.

"Uhh, your stripper just called and said she's at home with food poisoning. She ain't coming, man. She tried to call a friend to fill in, but she was unavailable too."

"Shit! So, we have no stripper?"

"Nope. Sorry. I could make a couple of calls and probably try to find someone else for you, though I can't guarantee the quality of a stripper so last minute."

"No, that's okay. He'll just have to deal with not having one. Thanks, man."

"No problem. I'll throw in a couple of rounds of drinks for you guys tonight. Sorry about the last minute cancellation. She's never done this to me before. She's usually pretty professional. Well, as professional as you can get for a stripper," he says as he walks out of the room.

"Well, that sucks," I mumble as I return to where my brothers are standing.

"What's the matter?" Nate asks.

"The stripper's not coming. Apparently, she has food poisoning."

"Well, that sucks! I was looking forward to that part the most."

"No shit! I couldn't wait for her to embarrass the hell out of Maddox."

The only redeeming part of this night now is thinking about what's going to happen when we make a surprise visit to the little room next door. There is one stripper still here who no one is expecting.

Chapter 14

Erin

We made our way to Jack's Pub and are now in the private small room in the back that I didn't even know was here. Around eleven thirty, there's a loud knock at the door.

"Avery, someone's here. Will you get the door?" Holly hollers in a singsong voice.

"Ugh! I can barely walk straight, Holly," Avery mumbles as she walks—or more like stumbles—toward the door.

When she throws open the door, a very large, very muscular cop is filling the entire doorway. Though he's wearing a hat, I can tell he has long, almost shaggy blond hair and huge muscles. Hell, his muscles have muscles. The exposed skin on his arms is covered in tattoos and his uniform is skintight. There's no hiding anything in that thing! I can't tell what color his eyes are because he's wearing Maverick from *Top Gun* style sunglasses, at night and inside a building, which is a huge indication of what kind of "cop" this man really is.

"Excuse me, ladies, but there have been a few complaints about excessive noise coming from this room. I'm going to have to come inside and get to the bottom of this," Mr. Hot Stripper says as he walks inside, closing the door tightly behind him.

"My fiancé is a cop," Avery slurs. "I know everyone, and I don't know you."

Hot Stripper grabs Avery's hand and leads her over to the chair that has mysteriously appeared in the center of the room. All eyes are now on the stripper and Avery, and huge smiles are spread across everyone's face in the room. Hell, even the moms have excited looks on their faces.

"I heard you have been a very naughty girl tonight. Is that true?" he murmurs in a sexy voice.

The proverbial light flips on at that moment, and Avery tries to bolt from the chair. "Oh, no, no, no, no. No! I know what you are! You're a stripper!" she exclaims as the stripper gently pushes her back down in the seat. From behind us, Holly flips on the stereo and the sound of Bruno Mars's "Locked Out of Heaven" fills the small room.

Avery's hands fly to her face, shielding her eyes as Mr. Hot Cop Stripper starts to seductively sway his hips, flipping his glasses off his face and ripping open his shirt. His chest is chiseled to perfection and glowing from the oil. He starts to straddle her lap and goes about shaking what his mama gave him all over her.

I glance around and see all eyes, including the eyes of the two mothers, glued to the show. Everyone is cheering Avery on, trying to get her into the performance a little more. I actually see Mrs. Stevens pull a few dollar bills out of her purse.

When the stripper takes a step back from Avery, he grabs a hold of his pants and pulls them away from his body in one quick, swift motion, leaving him standing before her in a skimpy, spandex G-string that reads, "Big Gun." He instantly goes back to moving and grinding on her lap, pulling his hat down low on his head in a sexy sort of way.

The stripper reaches down and grabs a hold of Avery's hand and gently places a pair of fur-covered handcuffs around her wrists. Her mouth drops open, practically all the way to the ground, and her eyes are as wide as saucers. He stands her up and continues to grind against her. When he bends her over gently, placing her hands on the chair in front of her, he actually pulls a paddle out of his bag-o-tricks and gives her a swat on the rear. She whips around to face him, eyes wide in horror. I'll admit; I'm actually a little embarrassed for her. I would be completely mortified.

When he sets her back down in the chair, Holly appears at her side with a handful of dollar bills. As the stripper continues to dance and gyrate on Avery, she decides to suck it up and take one for the team. She starts to stick a dollar bill inside his man thong the best she can, without actually touching him. I can't help but laugh at her facial expressions, which are a combination of concentration and horror.

After the song ends, Def Leppard's "Pour Some Sugar On Me" fills the room. Mr. Cop Stripper thanks Avery for being such a great sport, and starts to dance around the room toward the other ladies.

She rushes over to my side, still in handcuffs mind you, and throws her arms around my neck. "That was *so* freaking humiliating!" she exclaims.

"I can't even imagine!"

"Just you wait, missy! When you and Jake get married, I'm *soooo* embarrassing you just like that!"

Jake and I getting married? The warm, happy feeling settling in my chest actually kicks my heart rate up a notch or two. I could definitely consider a happily ever after with Jake. "No way! There will be no strippers at any party you may throw in the very distant future for me."

As the stripper makes his way toward me, I start to look for my exit. But Avery must anticipate my flight-risk status, and grabs a hold of my hand and pulls me toward her. She slaps a dollar bill into my hand as Mr. Stripper Cop turns around and sticks his dancing ass out at me. I can do this. I have on my big girl panties tonight. I can stick a dollar bill into a stripper's thong.

I reach forward and stick the dollar into the tiny strap just over the stripper's bare ass. Just when I'm letting go of the strap, he spins around and throws his big, broad body against mine and starts to grind. My face bursts into flames as the embarrassment takes over. I'm surprised I can even hear the catcalls and laughs of my friends over the buzzing in my ears.

Once he gives me a little show for my dollar, he moves on to Holly, who is standing on the other side of Avery. He continues until he's danced for each girl in the room, including the moms, who—I might add—stuffed way more than a single dollar bill in that man's thong.

After "Pour Some Sugar On Me" finishes, our entertainer turns and bows for the crowd. "Thank you, ladies. My name is Sam and it has been a pleasure to dance for you all this evening. Before I go, I have one more treat for our bride-to-be. Let me get completely dressed and I'll tell you all about the fun we're going to have, ladies."

The stripper stuffs his thong covered groin back in a pair of jeans and throws on a new black T-shirt from the duffle bag he brought with him. Once he has his shoes on, he walks over to Avery and sits her back down on the chair in the middle of the room and removes her handcuffs.

"Now, ladies. Our little bride-to-be is going to have a little more fun. I am going to take this here blindfold"—he bends down and removes a blindfold from his bag of tricks and starts to cover Avery's eyes—"and cover up her beautiful blue eyes. Can you see me, Avery?"

"Nope," she slurs.

"Then we're all ready to go. Our bachelorette here is now going to strip me—blindfolded—and give all of you ladies a great show!"

"Oh, no. No way!"

"Come on, Avery! You can do it," Holly cheers her on from her position next to me. While the stripper goes about trying to convince Avery to strip him, Holly leans over and whispers in my ear, "Watch this. You won't want to miss this!"

"I promise you, Avery. You are going to love this part," the stripper says as he goes over to start the stereo again.

Once Beyonce's "Single Ladies (Put A Ring On It)" starts up and Avery is sitting like a statue in the middle of the room, our stripper starts to walk toward Avery, when the door opens. The door swings opens and in walks Maddox.

Chapter 15

Jake

It's almost showtime. I'm pretty sure Maddox passed drunk a little while ago, and is well on his way to feeling like death for at least two days after this party. I'm also pretty sure he has no clue Avery is in the room next door. When Gabe opens the door and gives me the head nod—our sign to gather the troops for the next phase of fun—I walk over to Maddox and pull him aside.

"Having a good time?" I ask.

"The best," he slurs. "You're the greatest freeend ever!"

"Well, I have a little surprise for you, my friend. Avery's next door with the girls."

"She is?" His whole face lights up at the prospect of seeing his fiancée.

"She is, and I'm going to level with you. There's a stripper over there." I see Maddox's jaw get tense and tighten. "But here's the deal. Right now, she's blindfolded and thinks she's about to strip down the stripper. We want *you* to go over there and let her strip you. She won't know it's you until she removes the blindfold."

"I'll be damned if my girl is gonna strip a stripper. I'm in." We head toward the door, and I grab Nate to help gather all of the other guys in the group to come over and watch the show. "Wait. What if she actually strips me down? I don't exactly want my mom and future mother-in-law to see my junk."

"Dude, do you really think she's gonna strip you? You know how embarrassed she gets. That's the point. Let's go embarrass her a little and have some fun. She has no clue it's going to be you. You could even play along and egg her on a little," I respond with a smile.

When we get to the other door, Gabe opens it and signals for Maddox to walk in first. I'm right on his heels as we walk into the room and take in all of the very shocked faces of the girls in there. My eyes crash into Erin's and I'd say she's definitely shocked, but also afraid. Afraid of Maddox busting in on the bachelorette party when the stripper is performing, I assume. Some Beyonce song about puttin' a ring on it is blaring through the speakers.

Maddox actually strolls up to where Avery is sitting in the chair and grabs her hands, helping her to stand up. The stripper walks up behind him and over Maddox's shoulder says, "Okay, I'm ready. Strip me." Then he pats Maddox on the back, grabs his bag, and heads out the way we all just came in.

Avery just stands there so all the girls start encouraging her a little more. I quietly walk over to the side where Erin is standing and slide up behind her. I wrap my arms around her middle, leaning down and resting my chin on her shoulder, and inhale the tropical scent of her shampoo that I love.

"Hi."

"Hi," she says with a smile on her face.

"Having fun?"

"Yes. You?"

"Considering I can't drink, I actually am. I'm making sure he's having a great time," I say as I shake my head in Maddox's direction.

I look on as Maddox grabs a hold of Avery's hands and places them on his chest. He's smiling like the cat that ate the canary. I see Avery lean in slightly and her fingers flex over Maddox's chest.

Then all of a sudden, like someone flips the switch, Avery starts to slide up against Maddox. She rubs her hands up and down his chest, pawing and grabbing at him like a woman who was just given free rein to rub all over the man in front of her. She actually seems to be enjoying herself.

"She knows," Erin whispers over her shoulder into my ear.

"No way. How would she know?"

"Did you see her lean forward? She knows. That's why she's so into it all of a sudden. She knows it's Maddox!"

I turn back to my sister as she rips Maddox's black T-shirt forcefully out of the front of his pants. She slides her hands under his shirt, up his bare chest. Maddox looks shocked and a little alarmed, but I can see him shiver at the contact. I don't think he can believe she's actually doing it. But I give the guy a lot of credit, he remains perfectly still.

Avery pushes Maddox's shirt up and quickly pulls it over his head. She takes the shirt in one hand and spins it over her head before throwing it to the side. The girls are screaming their encouragements at her, and the guys are all wide-eyed and quietly laughing with their beers along the surrounding walls of the little room.

Avery starts to shimmy and shake as she rubs her front up against Maddox's chest. The look on his face is fucking priceless! When she steps back and dances to the beat of the music, she reaches down and grabs a hold of his belt buckle. She slowly starts to pull the belt end through the buckle until the belt is wide open. She whips it out of his belt loops in one fast, fluid motion that makes me wonder if she's done that before.

Everyone starts cheering and catcalling even louder. Avery takes the belt in one hand and turns around. She starts to grind her back against Maddox's front as she dances along with the music.

Maddox's eyes crash into mine and all I can see is the panic. Well, panic mixed with arousal. A lot of arousal. He mouths, "She's doing it!" to me.

I just nod my encouragement and quickly try to think about Avery being anyone else right now—my little sister is *not* dancing around and stripping a guy in front of me. Shit! Maybe I didn't think this through completely when Holly suggested it as a way to embarrass her.

Just then Avery turns around and grabs Maddox's pants. Her fingers wrap around the button on his jeans. Maddox looks like he's about to piss himself. He's pretty much standing in front of our entire family, our friends, and coworkers while his fiancée dances for him and strips him. But the funny thing is, as embarrassed as I'm sure he is, I can also imagine he's hard enough to break glass right now.

I smile at the display in front of me and hug tighter on Erin. When Avery pops open the button on Maddox's jeans and slides down the zipper, her hand lingers on his stomach over the top of his underwear. I can only pray that her hands stay above his underwear's elastic. Please for the love of God, she better keep that hand above his waistband! Avery continues to rub her hands up and down his chest, dipping them down lower and lower with each pass.

Just when I think we might get a little more of a show than we bargained for, Avery jumps up on her tiptoes and slams a hard kiss onto the very stunned lips of Maddox. Everyone bursts out laughing and cheering when she throws her arms around his shoulders and jumps up on his chest, wrapping her legs around his waist.

When he throws his arms around her, essentially holding her up, she reaches up and removes her blindfold. The ornery gleam in her eyes actually makes me pretty damn proud as big brother.

Maddox throws another kiss on her smiling lips while everyone starts to go back to drinking and talking.

"I can't believe you figured it out," Maddox says to Avery as they walk toward Erin and me, stopping to pick up Maddox's T-shirt on their way.

"How did you know it was him, Avery?" Erin asks with a big smile.

"I could smell him," she says with a smile as she gazes up at her fiancé.

"You could smell him?" I ask.

"Yep. He has a very distinctive smell. I could pick him out of a full auditorium if I had to," she replies with a little shrug of her shoulder.

"Holly! Did you know Avery could smell Maddox?" I yell over them as I shake my head in disbelief.

"No way," Holly says as she walks over and joins our conversation. "You really knew it was him? Did you peek?"

"No, I didn't peek! I knew it was him as soon as I stood up and he put my hands on his chest. I know this chest very, very well," she says with a giggle as she gives his bare chest a little rub. "So, since everyone else didn't know I knew, I decided to have a little fun with it."

"You were going to show everyone here, including our mothers, just how excited I was to have you rubbing all over me and stripping me. Three more seconds and everyone in this room was going to know exactly what effect you have on me," he says with a wolfish grin as he slides his T-shirt back over his head and refastens his pants.

"I wasn't going to go that far."

"That's a good thing for you because as soon as you would have pulled my pants down, all these girls would have been attacking me. You'd have to beat your friends off me with a big stick, babe."

"Oh, shit. Here we go," I say, rolling my eyes and shaking my head as I grab on to Erin's hand.

Maddox and Avery walk away laughing, heading to mingle with their party guests, while Holly heads over to get another drink, leaving Erin and I alone finally.

"So, what are your end of night plans?" I ask.

"I was hoping to find some hot guy to go home with tonight," she deadpans.

"Really?" I ask, eyebrow sky-high and a sly little grin on my face. "Maybe I can help you out. I just might happen to know a guy."

"Is he tall, dark, and devastatingly handsome?" she asks with a cute little grin.

"Definitely. I've even heard he has a thing for quiet redheaded librarians."

"Well, where is he?" she asks while looking around at the crowd. "Point me in his direction," she replies.

And because I can't help myself—I love messing around with her—I point down to my growing crotch. "Oh, don't you worry, darlin'. You'll be getting up close and personal with him later on when we're in private."

She laughs and turns her blushing face back to the party.

Later that night—or more like very early in the morning—after everyone is dropped off at their homes respectively, Erin and I head back to my place to crash.

"I think it was a successful party," she comments as we walk through the door.

"Absolutely. Maddox should be passed out already and, hopefully, up early in the morning puking his guts out."

"Oh, I bet he's not passed out yet," she says as she sets her bag on the floor and throws her coat over a kitchen chair.

"Why do you say that?" I ask as I do the same with my coat.

"I think Avery had a little something special up her sleeve for tonight," she says with a coy smile.

"If you're talking about sex, stop right there. I don't want to hear anything about what my sister and Maddox are doing right now."

A huge smile crosses her beautiful face. "I believe it has more to do with the fact that she found something special to wear tonight."

"And how might you know this?" I ask curiously. Do women really discuss their undergarments with each other? Like when they're in the bathroom together, since it's apparently illegal for a woman to go to the restroom without all of her girlfriends.

"I might have been with her this morning when she did a little shopping."

"Really?" Now I'm really curious. Avery and Erin went shopping together? For lingerie?

"Really. I might have even found something for you as a treat for being such a good boy tonight and not drinking," she says as she stands here looking all cute and shy. I want to grab her and kiss the shit out of her right now.

"I had not a drop to drink tonight, darlin'. Definitely a good boy," I say as I finally grab a hold of Erin's small wrist, pulling her against me. My need to touch her is so desperate that I can't even control myself. Mine. She's mine.

"Well, then have a seat on the couch, Mr. Stevens. You deserve a reward," Erin says as she leads me into the living room and gently pushes me back against the couch. I drop in the seat like my legs give out, a huge smile on my face as I sit anxiously awaiting whatever it is Erin has up her sleeve.

"Stay here. I'll be right back," she says over her shoulder as she grabs her bag and heads into the bathroom.

I'm already half hard as the different prospects flash through my mind. Erin bought something; I know it. I can't wait to find out what it is. I start to get a little antsy as I wait for Erin to come back out of the bathroom. My hands are jittery and my legs are both bouncing. Yeah, I'm damn excited!

When she comes out of the bathroom, I almost come in my pants like a teenager. Erin changed from her black sweater into a formfitting, white button-down shirt, a tight black pencil skirt and those sexy fuck-me pumps. She also has her hair up in a bun on the back of her head, and she's wearing her black-rimmed reading glasses. She is officially the world's sexiest librarian.

She walks over and turns on my stereo that is sitting in my entertainment center, flipping it to a station playing some sort of dance music. As she gets closer to me, I can see black lace through her white shirt. I grow painfully hard and am itching to jump up off this couch and grab a hold of her, throwing her down on the couch, but I know she has something up her sleeve so I remain seated and patiently, or more accurately, impatiently wait.

The look on her beautiful face tells me she's both excited and nervous as hell. I know that she's so far out of her comfort zone right now as she walks around like a damned wet dream.

When a new song starts, Erin starts to gently sway her hips in time with the music. Fuck me! She's going to dance! I watch the seductive sway of her hips as she begins to dip a little with the music as she moves back and forth. She closes her eyes as she lets the beat of the music take over her body and she places her hands on her thighs. I don't think it's possible to get any harder, but somehow, I manage. I'm afraid my dick might actually explode.

I sit back and watch—I couldn't take my eyes away from this if I tried—as Erin reaches up and slowly starts to unbutton the buttons on the shirt while she continues the slow, seductive moves of her hips. She does it slowly, so painfully slow, as she moves along to the beat of the music.

Once she reaches the bottom button on the shirt, she opens her eyes and I get a full view of what she's wearing underneath. It's the sexiest black-and-white lace bra I've ever seen. The lace leaves little to the imagination. My eyes burn hot as I stare at her beautiful chest and her nipples are actually growing into hard nubs under my intense scrutiny. I watch as she inhales sharply at the uncontrollable reaction her body has to my examination.

Erin slowly lets the shirt slip over her shoulders and slide down her arms, dropping it on the floor behind her, as she continues to sway seductively to the beat of the music. She slowly turns around and I'm treated to the view from behind. Her heart-shaped ass is accentuated perfectly in the tight, black skirt. She looks at me over her shoulder as she reaches around and slowly tugs on the zipper in the back of the skirt.

My eyes drop down to the curve of her ass, to the skin that she's exposing little by little, as she tugs the zipper down. When I see white and black peeking through the zipper opening, I almost leap up off the couch. She's going so damn slow it's killing me. I want to rip that skirt off her body so quickly, that I don't care what condition it would leave the skirt in when I'm done, and run my hands all over her body, from head to toe.

As she starts to shimmy and shake her hips, her hands pushing the skirt down her hips, I finally get a full view of what she has been hiding underneath that skirt. It's a combination of black lace and white satin boy cut panties. I can't control the loud moan that comes from my throat. I can't take my eyes off of her body. She's so fucking beautiful.

When she actually bends over and reaches down to touch her ankles, treating me to a full back view of her in those delicious panties, I'm on my feet before I even comprehend that I'm moving. I reach her as she looks over her shoulder at me, still bent over in that unbelievably sexy position, which has me so turned on I think I'm going to die if I don't touch her. Right. Now. Her eyes are wide and full of lust, her mouth open as she pants uncontrollably.

Erin quickly stands up and turns to face me. As I reach for her, she holds her hand out to me, palm straight out as if ordering me to stop. I immediately stop and stare at her, my eyes as wild as hers, I'm sure. She takes a step forward and places her hand flat against my chest, giving it a gentle shove, which causes me to fall back onto the couch again.

As I look up at her from my position on the couch, she walks over—still in her fuck-me heels, by the way—and stands before me with her feet shoulder-width apart, hands on her hips. Her hair is still up in the bun and she's wearing her reading glasses. If librarians ever actually looked like this, I would have spent more time in a library, that's for sure. But, I'm so damn glad she only looks like this now, with me in private. This wild, exotic Erin is for my eyes only! She's mine.

Erin reaches up and removes the clip from her hair, causing her red ringlets to tumble down around her shoulders. She gives me the most seductive smile as she reaches up and removes her glasses, throwing them aside on the couch. She then steps forward and places her knees on either side of my thighs, straddling me where I sit. My mind can't even begin to process what is happening. Aliens could land in the front yard, SWAT could storm my house, a tornado could rip this place to shreds and I wouldn't care in the least. All I care about, all I need, is to satisfy this uncontrollable desire I have to touch her, kiss her, and bury myself inside her all at the exact same time.

My hands wrap around her waist as I drag her forward so her center is rubbing against mine. I growl loudly at the friction created by the motions. I can feel the heat radiating from her center, I can smell her arousal, and it's driving me crazy. I grind myself against her and watch as her eyes flutter closed.

"I need to touch you, darlin'," I hear myself say.

"Touch me, Jake," she replies breathlessly.

My hands are everywhere: her hips, her ass, her stomach, her breasts. Erin grinds against my groin, causing us both to moan in torturous pleasure. I want to take this slow. I need to take this slow, or it will be over all too soon. She went through all this work to give me this show, the least I can do is to make this moment last for her.

I reach up and run my fingers along her lace-covered breasts, palming her breasts in my hands. I pull her chest against me, bringing her breasts up to my mouth. I devour her lace-covered mounds, sucking one inside my hot mouth. After I feast on one, I make sure to give the other equal attention.

I slowly drag the lace down to expose her hard peaks. I gorge on the vision before me, feasting on her breasts like I'm a man possessed. Erin arches her back, pressing down on our centers and forcing her breasts to my face.

My hands slide down her body and seek out the heat between her legs. I rub over her through the lace and satin. She's already soaked. Erin starts to grind herself against my hand as she seeks relief from the desire coursing through her body. I pull her panties aside and slide my fingers along her core, rubbing her wetness around. Erin moans loudly as she wiggles and shakes uncontrollably.

I slip one finger inside of her, watching the ecstasy on her face as it invades her body. I quickly add a second finger as my other hand grabs on to her hip, firmly holding her in place. I continue my assault on her wetness until I know she's ready to come. I back off and pull my fingers out, causing her to whimper at the loss of connection.

My lips finally seek hers as we crash in a fiercely hot kiss of lips and tongue. Without breaking the connection of our mouths, I push her hips up a little to get to my belt. One handed, I unbuckle my belt and unbutton my pants while she makes fast work at removing her panties and bra. Her hands dive down and she rubs my hardness through my jeans before she finally helps me pull my zipper down.

Once my zipper is down, I lift my hips and shimmy until my jeans clear my hips and thighs and are down around my ankles. I try bending forward and make a grab at my back pocket on my jeans for my wallet.

"No," she whispers against my lips. "I want to feel you. All of you."

My brain officially short circuits. I've never gone bareback before. Ever. But I have this irrepressible desire to do it now with Erin.

"I'm on the pill," she whispers. "And I'm clean."

I moan as I forego my quest to retrieve my wallet. "I'm clean too. I promise. I've never had sex without a condom before."

"Me neither," she says with a shy smile on her face as she rises up slightly on her knees, her heels scraping the outsides of my legs. I position myself at her entrance and stare deep into her green eyes as Erin slowly lowers herself down onto my rock-hard shaft.

I'm assaulted by her tightness, her warmth, her wetness. It's everywhere and I can feel it so completely that I'm utterly lost in the moment. I realize as I look up into Erin's beautiful emerald eyes, I am completely in love with her. I am so fucking in love with her that I can't think or see straight.

When I am completely inside of Erin, buried to the hilt, my lips latch on to hers in another smoldering kiss. She gently starts to move up and down, grinding down on me recklessly. I'm already so damn close to exploding inside of her, but I do everything I can to hang on a little bit longer.

After a few moments, her pace begins to quicken. She pulls away from my kiss and sits up, riding me with abandon. I'm mesmerized by the bounce of her breasts, the rise and fall of her hips. I feel her insides start to grip me so damn tightly that it pushes me completely over the edge. I grip her hips firmly as I hold on to her for dear life while she rides me. She screams my name as her release takes over her body, and I'm right there with her. I pump up into her a few times before my entire body goes limp with sweet release.

Erin falls forward onto my chest, our slick bodies sticking together, as we both struggle to catch our breath. I wrap my arms around her and close my eyes, breathing in her sweet scent and just enjoying the feel of her body against mine, surrounding me.

"That was amazing," she whispers.

"That was so much more than amazing. I don't think there's a word for it."

Erin chuckles and I feel her breasts press firmly against my chest. After I catch my breath, I gently pull back and out of her, losing our connection. I reach down and grab my T-shirt to use to aid in our clean up. I've never had to do this without just dropping the condom in the garbage. This way is a little messier but way better.

I also go to work on untying my shoes, kicking them off, and losing my pants. I leave them lying on a pile in the floor as I turn back to Erin, pick her up in my arms, and carry her toward my bedroom.

I lay her in the middle of my bed and climb in next to her. Once we're under the warm covers, I get as close to her as humanly possible. She's smashed against my side, head resting on my shoulder, and leg thrown over my leg. She sighs deeply as she relaxes in my embrace.

"I have no idea what got into you tonight, but that was the sexiest damn thing that's ever happened to me," I mumble.

She giggles against my chest. "Well, I think it was time for me to step out of my comfort zone a little. I'm glad you liked it."

"Liked it? Darlin, I almost stroked out when you started dancing. I'll let you do that anytime you want."

"I'll keep that in mind. Good night," she mumbles as sleep starts to take over.

I lean down and kiss the top of her head, as I rub my hand up and down her back. "Night, Erin."

As I listen to Erin's breathing even out in sleep, I realize that tonight was a turning point for both of us. Erin opened up to me like she's never done before and did something that was far out of the safety of her comfort zone. And I realized my heart is capable of loving someone who isn't my family. Erin. I love Erin. Now, I just need to figure out where exactly we go from here.

Chapter 16

Erin

Sunday afternoon brings my first official Sunday family dinner with Jake and his entire family. I'm honestly a little nervous at the thought of seeing all of Jake's family in their element at a small intimate family gathering.

As we make our way up the long driveway, I can't help but be in awe of the beautiful home at the end of the lane. There's grass and even timber everywhere. I couldn't imagine growing up in a place like this. I grew up in rooms that constantly changed and the view was never this beautiful. Even when I was in Rivers Edge in seventh grade, we had a house in the "city" part of town where you had neighbors on all sides. This place is calm. Peaceful. Serene. I really like it.

My thoughts drift to a large house, similar to this one, and the vision of children running and playing everywhere. I've always known I wanted a child someday, but when I imagine Jake in that picture now, I quickly realize I don't want a child, I want a ton. A ton of little Jakes running around the yard, playing games, and reading under the shade of a big oak tree. As long as Jake is a part of the picture, I want everything.

Last night after the party and my little strip show, I realized I want it all. I want it all, and I want it with Jake. Marriage. Family. Forever. My heart will never beat the same way again. When Jake was laid up in the hospital after being shot, I knew without the shadow of a doubt that I was in love with him. But last night, while I was securely tucked in his arms, was the first time I felt complete. I felt whole. I felt cherished and loved in return.

I had to stop myself from blurting it out in that comfortable moment while he was dozing off to sleep. However, if there's one thing I know, it's that Jake would have freaked out and pulled away from me. He isn't exactly a long-term relationship kind of guy. He said that himself—many times over. So, I know slow and steady is the only way to go with him or I risk crushing everything we're building.

Jake parks his truck next to Maddox's and comes around to help me down. Once we near the front door, we can hear all of the sounds of the large family inside, even through the closed door.

Once Jake opens the door and we step over the threshold, my senses are on overload. I see a large, open home full of family photos and mementos. I hear all of the guys in the living room, all trying to talk over the television and each other. I hear Brooklyn's giggles, and Avery and Mrs. Stevens talking wedding stuff in the dining room. I can smell what I can only describe as mouthwatering Mexican food. I can sense the happiness of family from within these walls. I feel their love.

"Hey, you guys," Avery says from the dining room table. "Come on in here."

I walk in the large dining room and give her a quick hug as Jake does the same for his mom and then sister. "What are you doing?" he asks.

"Last minute wedding stuff," Avery replies and dives back into the stack of wedding memorabilia spread out all over the table.

"Time for me to go say hey to the guys," Jake says as he leans in and kisses me on the cheek before hightailing it out of the room as quickly as possible.

"What can I help you do?" I ask as I take a seat at the table across from Avery and her mom.

"Here. Get to folding these programs for the ceremony, please," Avery says as she scoots a stack of paper across the table to me. "I can't believe this is my last weekend to finish everything up, *and* it's almost over!"

"What else do you need help with? I have some free time when it gets quiet at the library. I can help you with whatever."

"Oh, thank you so much for the offer. We're actually doing really well; I just can't help but stress a little and be a little dramatic."

"Well, the offer stands. If I can help, just call me."

"Thank you. I'll keep that in mind."

Thirty minutes later, all of the programs are folded as well as the place cards for the reception. "Mom, is the seating chart complete?"

"Sure is, honey." Mrs. Stevens looks over at me. "I have you seated next to Jake at Avery's table. I hope that's okay."

"Oh, sure. You could just put me wherever though. Don't create room for me at the head table. I'd be fine some other place."

"Oh, don't be silly, dear. There is plenty of room for you at that table with Avery and Maddox, Holly, Aiden, and Jessica. Jake's the only one that RSVP'd for two."

"He did?" I ask curiously. Didn't he have to RSVP like weeks ago?

"Of course he did. Why? Didn't he ask you?"

"Actually, no he hasn't. He always just assumes stuff. Drives me crazy," I mumble under my breath, but of course his mom hears me.

"Oh my God! I didn't give you an official invite because he told me he was going to ask you and to *not* worry about it! I'm going to kill him!" Avery exclaims with a huge exhale of frustrated breath.

"That's our Jake. He's always been a take-charge kind of guy. Even as a kid, he was the bossy one. It probably comes with being the oldest. You're just going to have to put your foot down and put him in his place when you need to, dear. I'm sure it won't take you too long to learn how to run the show without him realizing you, in fact, are running it and not him," Mrs. Stevens says with a sly grin.

Avery and I both laugh as we clean up our mess left on the dining room table, while Mrs. Stevens heads off into the kitchen to get everything ready for supper. Once our cleanup is complete, we join her to get dinner ready for the family.

The Stevenses' kitchen is large and inviting, much like the rest of the home. There's a small kitchen table in the corner of the room under a big wall of windows. I can picture Mr. and Mrs. Stevens sitting at the table with their morning coffee and watching the wildlife frolic in their backyard. A large island sits in the middle of the room with plenty of counter space for cooking. I can see Brooklyn, and maybe even small Stevens boys sitting on the counter and helping Elizabeth cook.

Dinner smells absolutely delicious. Mrs. Stevens pulls a big pan of chicken enchiladas out of the oven, while Avery and I go about getting all the taco ingredients out of the fridge and plates and utensils ready for the masses. I can definitely picture myself helping these women set up for family dinners every Sunday.

"Avery, go rally the troops. Dinner's ready," Mrs. Stevens says as she removes the taco meat from the stovetop.

As soon as Avery is out of the room, Mrs. Stevens turns and looks at me with a smile. "Erin, dear, I hope you know we are so glad you are here tonight. We think Jake is very special, and I'm just so glad he finally found a woman who sees it too. That boy has given me more sleepless nights than I can count over the past thirty-two years, but I knew, eventually, he would stop running and playing around with catty, shallow women and settle down with a good, down-to-earth woman. I knew when he was ready to fall in love, he would fall hard."

"Oh, Jake isn't in love with me, Mrs. Stevens," I counter, though probably trying to convince myself more than her.

"Elizabeth. And I know you don't believe that for a second.

It's written all over his face every time he's near you. He loves you, even if he hasn't told you yet. And that makes me the happiest mom in the world."

I swallow hard over the lump that has formed in my throat. A moment later, the kitchen is inundated with Stevens men all grabbing plates and diving into the food. Jake comes up behind me and wraps his arms around me, cocooning me in his warmth and protection.

Once Jake and I make plates, and I mean, I made a plate. I have no idea where I'm putting all this food, but it all looks so dang good. Then we head into the dining room to join the family. Conversation mostly centers on Avery and Maddox's wedding, but eventually everyone gets to the latest on their jobs and personal life.

"So, Erin, how is everything going at the library?" Michael asks from the head of the table.

"Really good. I've started a few after-school programs for teens, and I am revamping the children's programs that go on during the mornings. I'm focusing on programs to try to get more youth involved in the library."

"Well, good for you."

"Yes, I heard about a few of the new things going on there when I was getting my hair done Friday afternoon. Word on the street is that you've really taken the bull by the horns and are making solid improvements to the library," Elizabeth adds.

"I'm glad people are seeing the positive. It's been hard work, but well worth it," I reply.

"There are tons of positives. I've already been to the library more times recently than I was the entire time I was growing up here," Jake adds as he reaches over and squeezes my leg.

"If memory serves me correctly, the only reason you went to the library when you were young was to make out in the back," Maddox adds with a laugh, earning him a swat on the arm from Avery. "Not that I know anything about that, dear."

"I'm sure you don't," Avery quips as she tries to hide her

smile.

Once dinner is finished and the guys head into the kitchen to clean up with Mrs. Stevens, Avery takes me upstairs to her old room. "Come on, I want to show you something." When I step inside the room, she gently shuts the door behind us. Her stunning wedding gown is hanging from the open door of the closet.

"I can't stop touching it," Avery says, unable to contain the huge smile on her face. "Isn't it the most gorgeous dress you've ever seen?"

"It definitely is a beauty," I reply with a smile of my own. Just the dreamy, far-off look on Avery's face is enough to make you smile.

"I have something for you," she says as she goes over to the bed and starts opening up bag after bag. "Here," she says as she shoves a small blue-and-green bag in my hand.

"What's this?" I ask as I remove the tissue paper and pull out the long black box. I open the box and see a beautiful charm bracelet snuggled within the lining.

"It's just a little something to say thank you for all your help with the wedding. Well, that and for your friendship. You've done so much for me lately, and I just wanted you to know how much I appreciate it and you."

My eyes fill with tears. I don't ever recall receiving a gift from a friend before with the exception of major holidays like Christmas and birthdays. "Avery, you didn't have to do this!"

"Yes, I did. I want you to have it. Here, let me help you," she says as she takes the bracelet out of the box and starts to fasten it around my wrist. "There are a few charms I already picked out that remind me of you. There's a book, a star that says friend, a butterfly that says believe, and a tree to symbolize you are establishing your own roots. You can add whatever you want to it."

"I don't even know what to say," I reply hoarsely as I grab a hold of Avery's hands. "It's beautiful. Thank you so much for this. And for your friendship." I lean in and hug Avery as a few tears escape my eyes. She truly is a beautiful soul.

"You're very welcome, sweetie. I'm honored to have your friendship and help with my wedding. So, thank you."

After a few moments, Avery and I each wipe the tears from our faces as we head back down the stairs to join the rest of the family. The guys are all watching some sporting event on the television in the living room, and are apparently happy with a play. The entire room erupts into cheers.

Jake sees me coming down the stairs and jumps up, standing before me a moment later. "You're crying. What's wrong?"

"Nothing's wrong, Jake. Girls sometimes cry just to cry," Avery says with a smile before she goes into the living room to join Maddox and Brooklyn on the couch.

"What's wrong?" he asks, his voice laced with worry.

"Nothing, really. Avery just gave me this beautiful gift for helping with the wedding. I was really touched. I've never really had that kind of friendship before," I mumble as I hold up my wrist for him to inspect the bracelet.

Jake grabs a hold of me and pulls me in for a big hug. I find my comfort and peace while wrapped in his strong, capable arms. This might be my new happy place.

"You about ready to go? We both have to work tomorrow and I want to spend some alone time with you yet," he says with a little smirk.

"I'm ready," I reply as we head into the living room to say our goodbyes to the family.

The week literally flies by. Before I know it, it's Friday and everyone is gearing up for a weekend full of wedding festivities, which include the rehearsal and dinner tonight, wedding and reception tomorrow, and Sunday morning brunch at the Stevenses' for their family and the Jacksons. I'm closing the library early today, at three, so I can go home and get ready for the rehearsal.

I've stayed at my house more this week with Jake. He has been working more hours in preparation for taking the weekend off, so he usually comes by after work, I cook dinner, and we go to bed together, wrapped up in each other's arms after making love. I haven't told Jake that I love him yet, but know I want to tell him— soon. I need to say it for him and for myself, but know that getting those words past my tongue is going to be difficult.

Jake wouldn't be the first guy I've said the words to, but he would be the first person who I say them to and truly mean them when I say them. My ex-boyfriend, Tim, told me he loved me after three dates. It seemed like the right thing to do, to say, so I told him I loved him back. Even though Tim was a great guy who was career driven and goal oriented and a part of me really did love him, I never really felt the connection to him I feel with Jake. What I feel for Jake is all-consuming, all-possessing.

At three o'clock, I hear the front door open and close loudly. Hopefully, this is just a book drop-off or something that won't take too long.

When I step out of the small office, Jake is standing at the counter holding a calla lily, my favorite flower. A huge smile spreads across my face at the sight. He remembered my favorite flower? I told him on our first dinner date how my love for calla lilies came from my grandma after I moved in with her. She had a whole garden full of them in the backyard and spent hours trimming and pruning the bushes. So when she passed away, it seemed only fitting to order her favorite flower for her funeral.

"So, I was leaving the bakery just a few minutes ago and noticed the flower delivery truck across the street was unloading these. I figured they wouldn't miss one, so I grabbed it real quick while they weren't looking."

"What?! You did not!" I exclaim, horrified at the thought of a *cop* stealing a flower from the back of a delivery van.

Jake laughs. "Of course not. I'm a police officer. But I did see them in the truck and walk inside the floral place to buy it. For you," he says as he hands it to me over the counter.

The flower instantly goes up to my nose as I inhale this distinct floral scent that you only get from calla lilies. "Thank you. It's beautiful," I say with a smile.

"How much longer?"

"I have these couple of books to put away and then I'm done. Computer system is already down for the night," I say as I grab the small stack of books and head into the rows of shelves.

I make quick work on putting the books away in their rightful places on the shelves. As I start to slide the last book into place, I feel Jake's soft lips brush the sweet spot on the back of my neck and feel his hands wrap around my waist.

My head falls forward to allow him access to explore my skin further. His hands instantly drift up my shirt and his fingers fan out over my belly. My eyes flutter closed as I take in his hot breath and warm fingers caressing across my skin.

"Jake, what are you doing?" I whisper.

"I'm hoping to hit a home run in the library, Erin," he mumbles before his tongue snakes out to lick from my neck to my earlobe.

An uncontrollable shiver rips through my body as his tongue blazes a hot trail on my skin. "We can't do this here."

"Oh, but we can. I locked the door before I came back here. The lights are off and no one is around." Jake's hands dip down to the front of my dress slacks as he makes quick work of my button and zipper. The pants are sliding down my legs before I even process what's happening, not that I want to stop him anyway.

"I've been daydreaming about you all day, alone in this library, wearing those damn sexy glasses and this proper outfit. It's time to rip off these clothes and give me another taste of that naughty librarian I know is hiding underneath."

His words are like fuel to my fire as my body ignites instantly. I step out of my pants and make quick work on removing my panties. I can hear Jake's belt buckle and zipper sliding down and know that he's just as hurried behind me.

Once I'm bare from the waist down, I turn around to face Jake. The wild look in his eyes is a combination of desire and passion. He makes quick work of the buttons on the front of my blouse and dips his mouth inside to taste my exposed breasts.

After feasting on them for a few moments, his hands snake around my rear and he starts to lift me. "Wrap your legs around me, darlin'," he orders.

"Is that a question or a demand?" I ask breathlessly.

"A demand. Definitely a demand," he growls back as I wrap my legs around his waist, giving him exactly what he wants because it is, in fact, exactly what I want too. He's inside me in one quick thrust. Our moans mix together as our lips crash into each other. His pace and his kisses are swift and determined, and all I can do is hang on for dear life and ride out this wild ride.

It doesn't take long at all before I feel the familiar tightening in my lower stomach that only Jake seems to bring on. My legs tighten around his waist as he continues his rapid tempo, sliding in and out of me with fury. When he dips his head down and takes one of my nipples in his mouth, it's all over. I feel my core tighten around his shaft as I moan my release. The noises I make and the echoes throughout the library only seem to push him over the edge as he slams into me a few more times before stilling while buried deep inside of me.

I have no idea how he can still hold me up. My limbs are numb and weightless. My breathing is labored. My body is completely sated.

Jake leans forward and places gentle, tender kisses along my collarbone as he tries to get control of his own breathing. "That was so damn worth the wait."

"What?"

"Hitting that homerun in the back of the library," he says with a smile.

I laugh as I drop my jelly-like legs down and slide off of him. "Well, I'm glad I can be your first for something."

"Oh, believe me, you are," he says as he places a gentle kiss on my swollen lips. Before I can ask him what he meant by that, I hear his cell phone ringing in his pocket.

I start to dress quickly as he answers his phone. I'm able to figure out quickly that it's his mom on the phone as he goes about convincing her that we'll be ready and on time tonight. After I dress completely, I finally turn to look at Jake. He's standing there gloriously naked—well, with his pants down around his ankles—in the back of my library. It really is a beautiful sight, and I can't help but stare.

Jake hangs up the phone after a hurried goodbye to his mother and reaches for his pants. "Come on, we've gotta go. Mom is worried we'll all be late tonight and she's stressing. Apparently, Dad has gone for a drive to get out of the house for a little bit," Jake says with a smirk.

I start to head back to the office to get my coat, but Jake spins me around and into his strong arms. "That was unbelievable," he says against my lips.

"It was. Maybe we'll hit some balls at the library again real soon."

Jake laughs. "I think I've created a monster. I like it. I like it a lot."

Maddox and Avery's rehearsal went off without a hitch. I can't wait to see the whole ceremony unfold tomorrow. Brooklyn is a big part of the ceremony, and I know it's going to be wonderful as they finally become an official family of three.

The entire wedding party and immediate family is gathering at the small Italian restaurant in town. There's a private back room they allowed us to take over for the dinner, which Maddox's family is graciously covering.

The whole place has a dark atmosphere to it. The lighting is very low and there are small battery-operated candles on all the tables. There are red-and-white-checkered plastic tablecloths on all of the tables and Italian music softly playing through the speakers. It's a nice, quiet restaurant and usually draws a good crowd since it isn't overpriced like the big chain Italian restaurants.

I'm sitting between Jake and Holly during dinner. Jake keeps his arm casually rested on the backrest of my chair for most of the night, lightly rubbing my back or shoulders as he talks to his family. It's like his hands are magnets and my body is metal—they're just drawn to each other.

"So, Jake, are you getting married next?" Maddox's mother, Christine, asks casually.

I feel his arm stiffen against my back. Uh oh! "Well, I'm not planning on it right now, Christine. You never know what the future will bring though," he says casually as he goes back to lightly caressing my shoulder.

"Well, don't let this pretty girl get away, boy! It's time to settle down and get married. Look how long it took Maddox," Maddox's dad, Paul, adds.

Jake laughs nervously and I force a smile, all the while praying that someone changes the subject quickly.

As if sensing my discomfort, Mrs. Stevens chimes in, "Oh, Jake will get married when he finds that right person who will put up with him." Elizabeth smiles at Jake and winks at me before moving the conversation along. "So, Holly, how are things at the hospital?"

I completely tune out Holly's response as my mind races with more questions than I have answers for. Jake suddenly scoots his chair back and leans in to whisper in my ear. "I'll be right back, darlin'."

"Okay," I mumble, but he's already walking away from the table and heading for the restrooms down the hallway.

"I'll be right back," Travis says across from me as he scoots out his chair and heads toward the restrooms, following Jake.

A thousand things run through my mind at that moment. Is Jake mad? Does he think I have something to do with the marriage inquisition? What exactly does Jake's future hold? Am I in it? The questions just keep spinning round and round in my head like a record player. I feel the familiar ache of a looming headache start.

I decide a little air would probably do me some good, so I politely excuse myself and head toward the hallway. Just as I get ready to turn the corner, Jake's voice stops me in my tracks.

"Just do what I've been doing. Don't commit long term. Have a little fun for a while and then move on."

"I know it always works for you that way, Jake, but committing doesn't scare me. I stick with something once I start it," I hear Travis reply with a laugh.

My stomach literally falls to the floor and I feel like I'm going to throw up. Jake just confirmed to Travis that he's only with me for the temporary? To have a little fun until he gets bored or someone better comes along?

I back up a few steps and run into Avery. "What's wrong?" she asks, concern etched all over her face.

"Nothing."

"You look pale. Are you feeling okay?" Avery's "mom instincts" kick in as she steps toward me and tries to place her palm over my forehead.

"Actually, I'm not. I'm not feeling very well at all. I'm going to head out." I lean in and hug Avery quickly. "Will you tell Jake for me? He's busy talking and I don't want to interrupt him." I start to walk back toward the room where our dinner party is in full swing to retrieve my purse and coat.

"Wait! You're just leaving? Let me get Jake and he'll give you a ride home."

"No, that's okay. I'm only a couple of blocks away. The cool air will probably do me some good. I'll see you tomorrow," I throw over my shoulder as I head back into the room to get my stuff. I slip out quickly without anyone noticing, which makes me very happy. Well, as happy as you can be considering your heart was just ripped out of your body and stomped on by the guy you love.

I'm able to keep the rush of tears at bay until I reach the end of the block. When I round the corner and head in the direction of my house, the silent tears start to fall. I hug my arms against my chest as I walk, trying to keep it together. If I can just make it home, I can fall apart in private. I have been humiliated by Jake Stevens...again. And it's my own damn fault this time.

By the end of the block, I hear a truck approaching from behind and stop next to me along the side of the road. "Erin! Get in the truck," Jake yells through the downed passenger window.

"No thanks. I'm done taking orders from you."

"What the hell?" he says as he throws the truck in park and gets out. He's next to me in a few strides. "Erin. Seriously, what the hell is going on? Why did you leave? Avery says you're not feeling well?"

"No, Jake. I'm not feeling very well at all," I reply but keep walking.

"Get in my truck and I'll take you home if you're sick."

"Don't worry about it, Jake. Just go back to the party."

"Erin, I don't understand what the hell is going on here. Are you upset about something?" Jake asks as he steps in front of me and finally gets me to stop.

"No."

"Erin, don't lie to me. You promised you would always answer my questions when I ask. Darlin', what is going on?" Jake asks, concern etched on his beautiful face. A face that will haunt my dreams for the rest of my life. Jake was the one. At least he was for me.

"I heard you," I whisper.

"Heard me say what?"

"I heard you tell Travis to just have a little fun and then move on."

Jake looks up like he's thinking back to his conversation with Travis. "That wasn't about you, Erin," he replies defensively.

"Whatever, Jake. I'm done being humiliated by you. You just confirmed that you are the exact same person you were twenty years ago. A spoiled, selfish boy who only cares about getting what he wants; be damned with everyone else." I step around Jake and start to walk again toward my house.

"Erin, what the hell? Is that really what you think of me?" Jake asks but doesn't follow me.

I stop and turn back to face Jake. "It wasn't what I thought until about ten minutes ago. Until I realized the person I've come to care the most about in this world doesn't feel the same way. In fact, he feels the exact opposite."

Jake is staring at me, dark blue eyes burning into mine. "Well, then you better get home before this cold air freezes what's left of your frigid heart," he replies with his hands stuffed in the pockets of his jeans, face as hard as stone.

I turn around and walk away from him. My frigid heart? He was the one who admitted to only being with me until something better comes along. I was prepared to tell him that I was in love with him tonight, and I'm the one with the cold heart? No, the only thing wrong with my heart is the fact that it's shattered into a million pieces, and I don't know if I'll ever be able to repair the damage he's done.

The cool air chills my hot tears as I walk the rest of the three blocks toward my house. All I can think about now is curling up on my couch with Miss Whiskers and a pint of chocolate ice cream, and crying until there's nothing left inside except the ghost of a memory of Jake Stevens.

Chapter 17

Jake

Today is supposed to be a happy, joyous day. Today is supposed to be about new beginnings and celebrating love. But today just plain sucks.

I sat in my truck last night on the side of the road as the woman I loved walked away from me. I actually sat there and watched her walk those three blocks in the dark to make sure she got home okay, because as much as it hurt to have her rip out my heart last night, the thought of something happening to her on her way home was unbearable.

What the hell happened? One minute I'm talking with Travis in the hallway about someone asking him to join our softball league and the next thing I know; Avery is telling me Erin left because she didn't feel good. Something had clearly gone very wrong last night.

She obviously didn't hear the entire conversation last night in the hallway between Travis and me, but why she would jump to the ridiculous conclusion that I'm only with her to have a little fun for a bit until something better comes along, I have no damn clue. I would never do anything to hurt her. Ever. In fact, I was planning on having a very important conversation with her later this weekend.

Clearly, Erin isn't the person I thought she was either. She doesn't trust me and can't get over what happened twenty years ago. Fine. Whatever. I'm just glad I learned this now instead of when we're living together, engaged, or worse—married.

Yeah, for the past week, I'd actually considered all those things with Erin. I've imagined waking up every morning with her and not just because one of us stayed the night at the other's place. I want to wake up to her every day. Go to sleep with her every night. Plan things for our future—together. Well, I did. Hell, I still do.

When she accused me of that shit last night, I immediately jumped on the defense and said things right back, things I didn't mean. Erin has the warmest heart of anyone I've ever met. She's caring and generous and a damn good person. But, when she threw her past humiliation in my face, it made me realize that we might not actually get past that. And that hurt and scared me at the same time. So, I threw harsh words back at her and made her cry. I did the one thing I never, ever wanted to do. I made the woman I love cry. I really am a douchebag.

After I made sure she got home safely last night, I went back to the restaurant, even though I would have rather been anywhere else at that moment. I pasted on a big, fake smile and carried on like my life wasn't just demolished by the woman I love.

I didn't sleep a wink last night. Maddox slept over in my spare bedroom and tried to talk to me a few times last night about what was bothering me, but the last thing I wanted to do was burden my best friend on the night before his wedding with my own love troubles. So, I kept insisting I was fine and changing the subject.

This morning, the pot of coffee I just consumed won't even help. I'm tired and grouchy and really don't want to force fake smiles all damn day. But I won't be the guy who ruins his sister's wedding.

So, as I shave in front of the mirror in the bathroom, I give myself a little mental pep talk to try to help improve my mood. Unfortunately, my mind won't think of anything or anyone but Erin. The way she laughs. The soft curve of her neck. The way her lips part and her breathing becomes labored when she's aroused. All things that keep replaying on repeat in my mind like some scene from the movie *Groundhog Day*.

When I finally head into the kitchen, Maddox is sitting at the table drinking a cup of coffee. He looks rumpled in his T-shirt and lounge pants from sleep, hair in disarray, but he looks refreshed and ready for the day. "Did you sleep at all last night?" he asks.

"Nope."

"You ready to tell me what the hell is going on?"

"Nope."

"Obviously, this has something to do with Erin because I've never seen you this upset over anyone before."

"I'm fine. Besides, it's your wedding day. Let's talk about happy shit."

"My wedding day can wait, Jake. We don't have to be there for hours. Come on, man, talk to me."

I sigh heavily and take a seat across from Maddox. "She left last night after she overheard a conversation in the hallway between me and Travis. She only heard a very small portion of it, but it was enough to upset her and send her flying off the deep end with accusations."

"So, why haven't you set her straight?"

"I tried. She's assuming the worst about me and believes I'm only with her to fill time until someone better comes along."

"Ouch. I'm sure no woman wants to think they hear that; let alone Erin."

"What the hell does that mean?"

"Come on, Jake. Let's face it. In her eyes, you did something pretty horrible to her in the past, and she's scared you're doing the same thing again."

"I'm not!"

"I get that, but she feels like you've betrayed her all over again." Maddox takes a drink of his coffee and looks back up at me. "Let me ask you something. Do you love her?"

"Yes," I reply without even the slightest moment of

hesitation.

"Have you told her that?"

I exhale and shake my head from side to side.

"Why not?"

"We just never got to that yet. I was planning on telling her this weekend and even ask her to consider moving in together."

"So, you haven't told her you love her. She thinks she overhears a conversation where you're admitting to just wanting to have a little fun with her for awhile before moving on. You two have a major history, man. Hell, you haven't ever had a serious relationship and I get that, really, I do. I, of all people, understand that." Maddox pauses for dramatic effect. "Do you blame her for assuming you'd be that guy who was using her for a little fun?"

I can't even look at Maddox right now. I just hang my head in shame, running my hand over my weary face. I have fucked this up bad.

"You can't change what happened and what was said last night when you were upset. But you can change what happens from here on out. Don't be like me when I walked away from Avery. That is time I will never get back, and it was you who made me realize that," Maddox says as he takes the final drink of his coffee. "Come on. Let's finish getting ready for the day. We have lunch in a couple of hours with the guys at Jack's Pub, and then we have to be at the church to get ready. That leaves you with a little time this morning to decide if this mess is worth fixing or not. If it is, well then, go. Fix it." Maddox slaps my shoulder before he walks out of the room to get dressed.

He's right. I have to be at the Pub at eleven. That leaves me with three hours to go find Erin and fix this. I have to fix this because the thought of life without her isn't an option for me anymore.

My first stop is Erin's house. Of course, she's not there. Why would it be this easy, right? So, I hop back in my truck and head toward the library. I know she took the day off today, but maybe she stopped in to do some paperwork. Hell, maybe she decided to work the entire day. There's no guarantee Erin is going to show up for the wedding or reception today, so maybe she decided to work instead.

As I pull into the parking lot next to the library, I do a quick scan for her car, but I don't see it. I decide to go ahead and check inside, just in case. When I pull open the large door, I instantly see a young high school girl working behind the counter.

"Is Erin here?"

"No, I'm sorry. She's off today. Can I help you with something?"

"No, thank you," I say as I turn and head back out of the library.

Once back inside my truck, I decide to drive by her place one more time. Maybe she ran an errand or something earlier. As I approach her house, I see that I'm wrong. Erin isn't there.

I end up driving around town for the next hour and a half looking for her. I check every parking lot and street I can think of, hoping I'll spot her red VW Bug. No such luck.

At ten thirty, I realize it's almost time to go meet the guys for lunch. I return to my house to pick up the groom, grab my tux, and head to Jack's Pub—all with a heavy heart. It's still beating, but I don't know if this empty ache will ever go away.

When we get to Jack's, everyone is already there. We snag the large table in the back and order big greasy cheeseburgers and fries. Instead of beers, we all opt for soft drinks; no one willing to take a chance at pissing off one of the moms or Avery today.

"I'd like to propose a toast," my dad says as he stands at the head of the table. "Every father always wants the absolute best for their children. Whether it's a son or a daughter, you want them to find their happiness, their place in the world. Avery is my only daughter. She is my light, my world. She is the second woman I've ever really loved with my entire being. And she gave me my first grandchild. She is beautiful, strong, and intelligent. She is caring and giving and forgiving. She is one of my five greatest joys in this world. And now, I am about to share her with you, Maddox. I couldn't be prouder or more honored to share with you my greatest joy. Not only are you getting a treasure, but she's getting one in you too. I can only hope when the time comes for my boys, they find the perfect friend and lover that you and Avery have found in each other. You're a good boy and I'm very excited to welcome you, officially, to the Stevens family. So, everyone, raise your glasses and toast to Avery and Maddox. Cheers!" Dad raises his glass and takes a drink of his ice tea.

"To Maddox," I say and truly mean it. I take a drink of my Coke and slap my best friend on the back. My dad's words bounce around in my head like a ping-pong ball in an arcade game.

I've already found her, Dad. I've already found her.

It's almost showtime and Maddox is starting to pace around the room we're all in at the back of the church. After I finished getting him dressed because the guy's hands were shaking so bad and he was working on his fourth try at tying his necktie, there's a knock on the door.

"Come in," Maddox says, nerves evident in his voice, as he rubs his sweaty hands up and down his suit pants for the tenth time.

My mom walks in and gives a beautiful smile to the room. She looks amazing and half her age in her beautiful lavender dress. Maddox, his brother, Aiden, my brothers, and I are all dressed in dark gray suits. The whole event is pretty small with me serving as best man and Maddox's brother as his groomsman. My three brothers are ushers.

"Look at this room full of handsome men," my mom coos with a big smile.

"How are the girls doing, Mom? Is Avery ready?" Will asks.

"They're all ready to go," she says with a big smile to the room before turning her attention to Maddox. "It's almost time. I just wanted to come and give you a hug and tell you how happy I am that you're marrying my daughter. And with the adoption looming around the corner, you've made me the happiest mother in the world today," Mom says with tear-filled eyes as she gives Maddox a big motherly hug.

"Thank you, Mrs. S., I won't ever let you down. I promise," Maddox replies. I decide not to draw attention to the fact that he takes a swipe at the moisture in his eye.

"I know you won't, dear. Now, if you boys will excuse me, I'd like to have a word with Jake in the hallway."

Mom walks out the door and stops just outside of it in the hallway; I follow her and close the door tightly behind me. My body is filled with tension, and I can sense the lecture coming. It's just like I'm the fifteen-year-old boy again who convinced Nate to climb on the roof and drop water balloons on Avery and her kindergarten friends playing in the backyard.

"Have you talked to her?" she asks with a knowing look on her face, arms crossed firmly over her chest.

I don't even have to ask who she's referring to. Mom always knows. "No," I reply and look down at my shoes.

"Why not, Jake?"

I exhale deeply. "I couldn't find her this morning. I looked everywhere: her house, the library, and just about every place I could think of in town."

"You didn't check your parents' house."

I look up at my mom. My eyes clash into the striking blue eyes that are identical to my own.

"Yes, she's been at our house all day. She arrived just before nine when all of the girls were gathering for brunch. I took one look at her and knew something more than just 'being sick' was wrong with that girl. She looked like she hadn't slept a wink and she was dying inside. So why don't you tell me why she has fought tears almost the entire day today?"

I close my eyes as the image of Erin crying invades my mind again. "I said something last night that I didn't mean. Something in the heat of the moment that I can't take back now."

"Does this have anything to do with why she left suddenly last night and you came back looking like someone ran over your dog?"

I exhale. "Yeah. I caught up with her down the road from the restaurant. She overheard part of a conversation and what she heard didn't exactly paint me in good light, so she took off and walked home. But, I swear, Mom, that conversation wasn't what she thought it was."

"Did you tell her that?"

"Of course! But she threw it back in my face. Said that I was spoiled and selfish and was only out to hurt her again. I didn't *do* anything wrong!"

"What did you say after she accused you of those things?"

"I...I basically told her to get stepping and not to come back," I say in a quiet voice as I hang my head in shame. "But I didn't mean it, Mom," I say, eyes pleading with her to believe me.

"Of course you didn't, honey. You know, there was a time right after you and Nate were born when your father and I fought all the time. It didn't matter what it was about or how frivolous it was, we fought and fought. One night, after one particularly horrible fight where we both said things we didn't mean, your dad stormed out of the house and tore out of the driveway in his truck. He was gone for over an hour and I started to wonder if we would actually make it to celebrate another anniversary. I cried for what felt like a lifetime that night, while I waited to see if he was coming home or not. Just when I decided to give up and go to bed, I heard his truck pull into the driveway. His boots were heavy on the steps and I was dreading the inevitable confrontation that was surely coming. But when your dad stepped through the front door and I took one look at his red, swollen eyes and his dirty, tear-streaked face, I completely forgot what we were even fighting about to begin with. I realized it was nothing compared to our relationship—*that* was worth fighting for. He pulled his hand out from behind his back and had a big bunch of wildflowers from a country ditch. They were the most beautiful flowers I'd ever seen or received. It was in that moment I realized your father and I still had a lot to learn about each other and ourselves, but as long as we were in it together, we'd figure out a way." Mom stares at me intently and reaches up to touch my cheek. "It's not what you fight about that matters, Jake. It's what you fight *for* that's really important."

I stare at my mom and throw a kiss down on her cheek. "You are the smartest person I know," I say with a smile.

Mom laughs and glances over my shoulder. When she makes eye contact with me again, she leans in and says, "Remember. It's what you fight *for* that matters, Jake." Then, Mom leans way up on her tiptoes, kisses me on my cheek, and turns and walks away.

I glance over my shoulder and see the most beautiful, breathtaking sight. Erin is standing in the hallway behind me wearing the most stunning navy-blue dress I've ever seen. The sight of her takes my breath away, and I'm rendered speechless. The look on her face shows her nerves, her fears. I want nothing more than to run to her and sweep her up into my arms. But I need to wait. I have a few things I need to say first.

Chapter 18

Erin

I am scared to death as I walk up behind Mrs. Stevens and Jake. My heart feels like it might actually jump out of my chest and start running around on the ground at my feet. He hasn't seen me yet, but Mrs. Stevens knows I'm here. She sort of had a hand at making sure Jake was in the hallway at this exact moment so we could talk before the wedding. I see her give Jake a kiss on the cheek and turn and walk away. It's just Jake and me in the hallway now.

When he turns around, my heart stops. Literally. He's so devastatingly handsome in his suit. I'm so excited to see him standing in front of me, but I can't help but wonder if he's at all happy to see me. Will he tell me to get lost? I have no clue, and I'm afraid of what comes next.

I slowly walk toward Jake, my eyes locked on his the whole time. His face gives nothing away to how he's feeling. "Hey," I finally say as I bite down on my bottom lip.

"Hey."

"Listen, Jake, I need to apologize—" I start, but Jake cuts me off.

"No. You don't need to apologize. I need to apologize and explain the conversation you overheard. Travis was asked to join the men's softball league this summer. I did it last year and loved it, but with working every other weekend, it made it difficult and I had to have my own replacement every time I worked. I was telling him to enjoy it for a while and then move on to another hobby if this wasn't his thing. That's all. I wasn't talking about you or any other woman, I swear to you, Erin."

"I know," I whisper as I take another step forward. I could reach out and touch Jake if I wanted, and man, do I really want to.

His brows wrinkle and his face takes on a confused look. "You do?"

"Yeah, I do."

"How?"

I give him a small smile as I answer. "Because I don't believe that's who you really are. I don't believe you would have intentionally said those things to hurt me. Even though I said it, I don't believe that you're using me until something better comes along."

"I'm not, Erin. At all. And what I said last night on the sidewalk..." Jake pauses and closes his eyes as if pained by the thought of what he said last night. "That was the farthest from the truth. You have the kindest, purest heart I've ever known. You make me want to be a better man."

"You are a better man, Jake. To me, you are the best man, and I'm not referring to the wedding. A very wise woman once told me that fighting meant passion and that you were alive. Fighting represents desire and love. You are the man I want to be with. You're the man I've fallen in love with," I say, my voice dropping to just above a whisper as I say the words I've wanted to say for almost two weeks now.

I wait for what feels like forever for Jake to reply, smile, nod, acknowledge what I said—something!

"Did you just say you love me?" he asks with that "I'm a cop and give nothing away" look on his face.

"Yes," I whisper so quietly *I* almost don't hear it. I'm silent as

I wait for him to say something, anything. I start to brace myself for the pain that is about to grab a hold of my heart. Fear that my love is not reciprocated grips me tightly in my chest and makes it nearly impossible to breathe.

"That actually works out really well for me, because I am so fucking in love with you too. I love you so much I can't imagine fighting with anyone else. It's you, Erin. You're the one," Jake says as he closes the gap between us and pulls me into his arms. He latches on so tightly, picking me up, hanging on to me like he's afraid to ever let go.

Jake's lips are on mine before I even have time to properly process what he just said to me. It has only been twenty-four hours since I felt his lush lips on mine, but it was the longest twenty-four hours of my life. I need Jake like I need air. And now that I'm back in his arms, I feel like I can finally breathe again.

The kiss is intense and passionate as we both try to convey our feelings in that one, simple gesture. If I could kiss this man for the rest of my life, I would die happy and know I was loved. I'm loved. I feel it in his kiss. The thought wraps around me like a warm blanket, enveloping me in its heat and tenderness.

"Excuse me, you two. I'm supposed to be getting married in a few minutes. Would you mind holding off on the dry humping until after the ceremony?" Maddox asks through the now open doorway with a smug smirk on his face.

"I was not dry humping her. I was just telling her how much I love her," Jake says with a smile as he gazes down into my eyes.

"Well, it's about damn time, man. And speaking of time, it's almost time! Where are those flower thingies we're supposed to put on?"

"Oh! The boutonnieres! I've got to get those pinned on you guys before you go out. Come here," I say as I tug Jake back in the room.

When the boutonnieres are in place and I've made sure everyone is lined up in the foyer and ready to walk down the aisle of the church, I turn to head inside the quaint little church to find a seat. Before I can get inside though, Jake grabs my hand and brings it up to his mouth.

"I'll see you in just a little bit, darlin'."

"I'll be here."

"Good. I have a dance saved later just for you."

"You better have all of them saved for me," I reply with a coy smile.

"Every last one of them from here on out is yours."

I smile at Jake and place a gentle kiss on his sweet lips before heading inside the church to find a seat. Nate escorts me to the front, a row behind where Mr. and Mrs. Stevens will be sitting. "Oh, I don't have to sit up here. It's for family," I whisper in Nate's ear.

"Mom gave me very specific instructions that you are to sit right here," he says with a small smile and a wink.

I take my seat just as the slow, instrumental music starts up. All eyes turn to the back of the church as Maddox's parents are escorted to their seats in the front row, followed by a beaming Mrs. Stevens. Moments later Maddox, Jake, and Aiden make their way up to the front of the church. Jake throws me that cocky half-smile that I love so much and a wink. I can't help but smile ear to ear as I stare back at him. Jake Stevens. The man I love.

As the music changes to "Canon in D," I turn back to watch Jessica and Holly make their entrance into the church and toward the front altar. Brooklyn comes in next in the most beautiful little white dress carrying a basket of rose petals. Her hair is pulled up on top of her head with little white flowers pinned in it. She looks every bit of the little princess she is.

Brooklyn takes one look at the audience in the church and starts to get a little shy under the scrutiny of the people. She stops halfway down the aisle and looks as if she's about to turn around and head back the way she came. Out of the corner of my eye, I see Maddox walk down the steps in front of the altar and start to approach Brooklyn.

"Brooklyn," Maddox whispers, squatting as he gets to the first pew.

Brooklyn turns back toward the front and sees Maddox standing there. Her entire face lights up with delight. "Daddy!" she exclaims and then takes off running toward him.

Maddox scoops her up in his arms and places a kiss on the top of her head. When they make it back up to the altar, the music changes again and everyone rises to stand. Maddox points down the aisle toward the back, indicating for Brooklyn to watch the back door.

When Avery and her father walk inside the church, I can't help but turn and watch for Maddox's reaction. His face lights up like a toddler who just discovered a room full of presents on Christmas morning. He holds his new daughter in his arms as his future wife walks toward him.

I look up at Jake next and see him looking at me with those piercing blue eyes. He's staring at me, his face carrying a sexy smile, eyes filled with desire, and I can see the love radiating from him. Tears fill my eyes again as I stare into Jake's blue eyes and return his smile. I don't question it or fight it. I just go with it because there is no one else in this world who I would rather be with. Love. Fight with.

Besides, a wise woman once told me the fighting is only the first, small step. The making up afterward is the best part.

Epilogue

Jake

I sit back and watch Avery and Maddox spin around the warmly lit dance floor. Tonight turned out to be one hell of a night. It doesn't even bother me that I smiled for what felt like a thousand photos. The wedding was perfect, the dinner delicious, and now my girl is sitting next to me, snuggled under my arm, as we watch my sister and my best friend share their first dance as husband and wife.

Husband and wife. Tonight is the first night the thought of it doesn't scare the living shit out of me. I see the way Avery and Maddox look at each other, and I realize I want that too. I want that with Erin. Only Erin. She is my sunlight on a dark day. She is my heaven on earth. She is my everything. Forever.

I look over at my brothers, sitting at the table with my parents, and notice Travis looking off in the opposite direction of the dance floor for like the twelfth time. When I follow his gaze, I see that same pretty server he's been staring at half the night. She has long brown hair pulled back in a neat ponytail, a white, fitted long-sleeved shirt, and black dress pants, just like the rest of the servers. I'm guessing she's somewhere between Avery's and Travis's age but has a very tired, worn-out look to her. Even when she smiles, you can tell she's exhausted. Appearance wise, she looks exactly like all the other servers walking around tonight. But for some reason, my brother hasn't taken his eyes off of her. I watch as Travis continues to observe the pretty girl while she works. I can't help my cocky little smile as he practically falls out of his chair when she approaches their table to collect glasses and empty beer cans.

Nate gets up and comes over to our table to sit in the seat Maddox just vacated a few moments ago, when he was summoned to the dance floor to dance with his new wife. "What's up, dickweed?" he asks.

"Nice. You kiss your mother with that mouth?" I reply with a smile.

"Every time I see her. So, what's this I hear about Travis taking your spot in the softball league?"

"Yeah, well he has the free time on the weekends and I don't. With working every other weekend, he was practically on that team anyway when he filled in for me. I'll still go and watch, maybe fill in when I can, but it was time to step back."

"I hear ya."

"Speaking of Travis, what the hell is up with him and that server?"

"No clue. He thinks he's being all sly and shit about watching her, but it's obvious that he's into her. He hasn't taken his eyes off her all night."

"That's what I was thinking. Good for him. Maybe he'll actually do something other than work all the damn time."

"You have no room to talk, Brother," Nate says as he takes a pull from his beer bottle. "You work and play all the damn time too."

"Yeah, I did." I look down at Erin, who is wrapped securely in my arm. "But I'm done playing. Time to grow up, you know?"

"No. I don't know," Nate says with a shake of his head and a laugh. "I'll keep on playing, if you don't mind."

"Suit yourself, man."

A new slow song starts and the DJ encourages everyone to come join the new Mister and Missus on the dance floor. I grab a hold of Erin's hand and gently tug her upward onto her feet. "Come on, darlin'. Let's go dance."

"Is that a question or a demand?" she asks with a smile as she follows me out onto the dance floor.

"It's a demand. I'm not giving you a chance to get away from me or tell me no," I say with a smug smile.

"Well, then you have nothing to worry about. I'm not going anywhere, Cowboy," she says as she reaches up, way up, and wraps her arms around my neck.

I pull her tightly against my body and just revel in the feel of her against me. I can tell instantly the moment she feels the effect she has on me—on my lower body. The desire filling her eyes makes me pull her even closer, which really isn't the best way to try to alleviate a raging hard-on. Especially since I'm in the middle of the dance floor surrounded by family and friends.

"So, I was thinking about later tonight," I begin.

"What about it?" she asks with her head resting on my chest.

"After the party is over and we leave. Where would you like to go?"

Erin looks up at me as she answers with a knowing smile, "Well, as long as there's a bed and *you* are in it with me, I don't really care much."

"See, that's kind of what I was thinking about. I thought maybe we could go back to your place tonight, and then maybe pick a place that we both go back to...every night. Together."

The surprise is evident on her face, but it doesn't take long for her smile to spread and light up her entire face. I know the question was a good surprise. "Are you asking me to move in with you?"

"Sure am. You can move into my place if you want, but honestly, it's pretty small. Your place is big and would give us plenty of room, but I don't want to just invite myself to move in with you. We could also find a new place, the perfect size for both of us."

"Does Miss Whiskers get to come too?" she asks.

"I wouldn't think of not taking your cat with us. But I think we need to rename her. I don't think me calling her Miss Whiskers is very manly, and I don't want to lose my man card."

Erin laughs and it's the most beautiful sound in the whole world. "Well, we wouldn't want that! But I'm afraid her name is Miss Whiskers. So, you're just gonna have to suck it up, big boy."

I smile down at her. "Fine. I'll compromise on the cat's name. Just as long as I get my other requests."

"And what are they?" she asks.

I lean down so my lips are against her ear. "Sex. Every night. And you also have to wear nothing but those damn glasses and sexy high heels at least once a week."

Erin throws her head back and laughs hard. "Deal," she says with a wink.

I pull her back against my chest and hold on tight. I've never really been a big dancer, but with her in my arms, I would gladly do it for the rest of my life as long as she was my partner. Erin in my arms, by my side, completes the puzzle inside of me. She is the piece that has been missing from my life; my heart. My heart belongs to her, and probably always has, since the moment I walked into the front office and saw her standing there in seventh grade. Now, I get to spend the rest of my life loving and fighting with the only woman I've ever loved; ever loved to fight with and fight for.

I can't fucking wait.

~ The End ~

Still need more Rivers Edge?

Start at the beginning with Trust Me, free on all retailers, <u>HERE</u>!
Or grab the next book in the series, Expect Me, Rivers Edge book 3, <u>HERE</u>.
The Rivers Edge series is now in Kindle Unlimited.

Don't miss a single reveal, release, or sale! Sign up for my newsletter.

http://www.laceyblackbooks.com/newsletter

About the Author

USA Today Bestselling Author Lacey Black is a Midwestern girl with a passion for reading, writing, and shopping. She carries her e-reader with her everywhere she goes so she never misses an opportunity to read a few pages. Always looking for a happily ever after, Lacey is passionate about contemporary romance novels and enjoys it further when you mix in a little suspense. She resides in a small town in Illinois with her husband, two children, adorable black lab puppy, crazy cat, and three rowdy chickens.

Website: www.laceyblackbooks.com
Email: laceyblackwrites@gmail.com
Facebook: https://www.facebook.com/authorlaceyblack
Instagram: https://www.instagram.com/laceyblackwrites/
Bookbub: https://www.bookbub.com/authors/lacey-black
Amazon: https://www.amazon.com/Lacey-Black/e/B00MW2UGZI
Twitter: https://twitter.com/AuthLaceyBlack
Goodreads: https://www.goodreads.com/author/show/8414783.Lacey_Black

Sign up for my newsletter so you don't miss a single sale, reveal, or release!
http://www.laceyblackbooks.com/newsletter

www.ingramcontent.com/pod-product-compliance
Lightning Source LLC
Chambersburg PA
CBHW060642260626
47161CB00008B/2958